The Laws of Evening

stories

Mary Yukari Waters

SCRIBNER

NEW YORK   LONDON   TORONTO
SYDNEY   SINGAPORE

SCRIBNER
1230 Avenue of the Americas
New York, NY 10020

SCRIBNER and design are trademarks of
Macmillan Library Reference USA, Inc., used under license
by Simon & Schuster, the publisher of this work.

For information about special discounts for bulk purchases,
please contact Simon & Schuster Special Sales:
1-800-456-6798 or business@simonandschuster.com

Designed by Kyoko Watanabe

Text set in Garamond 3

Manufactured in the United States of America

1   3   5   7   9   10   8   6   4   2

Library of Congress Cataloging-in-Publication Data
Waters, Mary Yukari.
The laws of evening : stories / Mary Yukari Waters.
p.   cm.
Contents: Seed—Since my house burned down—Shibusa—Aftermath—
Kami—Rationing—The laws of evening—Egg-face—The way love works—
Circling the hondo—Mirror studies.
1. Japan—Social life and customs—Fiction.
2. China—Social life and customs—Fiction. I. Title.
PS3623.A869 L3 2003
813'.6—dc21   2002029429

ISBN 0-7432-4332-3

Portions of this collection have been previously published as follows:
"Seed" in *Shenandoah*, reprinted in *Acorn Whistle, The 2000 Pushcart Prize*, and
*The Pushcart Book of Short Stories: The Best Short Stories from a Quarter-Century of the
Pushcart Prize;* "Since My House Burned Down" in *Glimmer Train Stories;*
"Shibusa" in *Triquarterly;* "Aftermath" in *Manoa*, reprinted in *The Best American
Short Stories 2002;* "Kami" in *Black Warrior Review;* "Rationing" in *The Missouri
Review;* "The Laws of Evening" in *The Indiana Review;* "Egg-Face" in *Zoetrope:
All-Story*, reprinted in *Prize Stories 2002: The O. Henry Awards.*

For my mother,
my father,
and
my grandmother

Acknowledgments

I am greatly indebted to my friend and mentor Tom Filer, who has not only guided my writing with love and expertise, but also opened up my life in many ways. Thank you also to the members of Goat Alley for their years of encouragement, advice, and excellent food; Tod Goldberg, for his generosity; and Michelle Latiolais, Geoffrey Wolf, and my teachers and classmates at UC Irvine's MFA program.

I owe a great deal to the National Endowment for the Arts, the Corporation of Yaddo, the MacDowell Colony, Hedgebrook, the Humanities Center at UC Irvine, the Barbara Deming Memorial Fund, and the Gerard Fellowship for recognizing and supporting my efforts when I needed it most.

Thank you to Joy Harris, who is everything I could hope for in an agent, as well as to Stephanie Abou and Alexia Paul. And thank you to my editor Gillian Blake, Rachel Sussman, and the rest of the team at Scribner, for their heartwarming enthusiasm and dedication.

Contents

The Laws of
Evening

Seed

THE NAKAZAWAS were in China barely a week when they first heard the drumming of a prisoner procession. They were sitting side by side on the hard seat of their new Western-style garden bench. Although it was twilight and turning cool, the ornamental wrought iron retained the sun's rays, reminding Masae of a frying pan slowly losing heat. Turning her head toward the sound, she stared at the concrete wall as if seeing through to the dirt road on the other side.

Clearly a small drum, it lacked the booming resonance of taiko festival drums back home. *Tan tan tantaka tan, tan tan tantaka tan,* it tapped in precise staccato, flat and toylike, as if someone were hitting the drumhead with chopsticks. Moments later, like an afterthought, came the scuffling sound of many feet, and a man's cough less than ten meters away. The Nakazawas sat unmoving in the dusk. Out of habit, Masae's thoughts darted to their baby girl: indoors . . . noise didn't wake her . . . good. Above the wall, in sharp contrast to the black silhouette of a gnarled pine branch, the sky glowed an intense peacock blue. It seemed lit up from within, some of the white light escaping through a thin slit of moon.

"Ne, what'll they do to them?" Masae asked her husband, Shoji, once the drumbeats began to fade.

"Shoot them, most likely," Shoji said. He shifted forward on the hard iron seat and leaned down to tap his cigarette with a forefinger, once, twice, over his ashtray in the crabgrass. "Some might get sentenced to hard labor."

Masae turned her entire body to face her husband's profile. Its familiar contours, now shadowed by nightfall, took on for an eerie instant the cast of some other man: hollowed cheeks, eyes peering from deep sockets. "Araa—" She sighed with a hint of reproach. Granted, these things happened in occupied countries and they had known about the prison camp before their move; still, they could do without such reminders while relaxing in their own garden. Masae wondered what people back home would think of this. In their old Hiroshima neighborhood, mothers went to great lengths to shield their children from unpleasantness, even pulling them indoors so they wouldn't watch two dogs circle each other in heat. Last winter, naturally, the neighborhood children had been spared any specific details of the Pearl Harbor incident. "I think," she now told her husband, "this is not a good location."

"H'aa, not so good," Shoji said. He sounded humble; normally he would have been quick to point out that the company had chosen this house. They sat silent in their walled-in garden, on the bench which had by now lost all its heat. Masae could sense a faint shift in their relations. The drumbeats still rang faintly in her ears, like the aftermath of a gong. In the mock orange bushes behind them, a cricket began to chirp— slow, deliberate, unexpectedly near.

"Ochazuke might taste nice," Masae said, "before bed." Comfort food from home: hot green tea poured over leftover rice, flavored with salty flakes of dried bonito and roasted seaweed.

"Aaah! Masae, good thinking!" Shoji said, rising. His hearty exclamation was absorbed efficiently, like water by a sponge, into the silence of the Tai-huen plains.

The Nakazawas lived two kilometers from the main town, which was so small it had only six paved streets. If Masae looked out from the nursery window on the second floor (for she rarely ventured past the garden walls), she saw the dirt road leading straight into town. To her left were hills: wheat-colored, eroded over centuries to low swells on the horizon. Dark wrinkles wavered down their sides, as if the land had shriveled. Right behind those hills, the Japanese Army had built a labor camp for Chinese prisoners of war. On the other side of the dirt road, a flat expanse of toasted grass stretched out to a sky that faded in color as it approached the earth, from strong cobalt blue to a whitish haze. Somewhere past that skyline was the great Pun'An Desert.

Shoji was not in the Army. He managed a team of surveyors. His company back home, a construction conglomerate, had targeted this area because there was talk of building a railroad; Tai-huen might become a crucial leg in the Japanese trade route. Similar foresight in the Canton and Hankow provinces, which had come under Japanese rule four years ago, in 1938, was paying off now in housing commissions. "The faster we take the measurements," Shoji kept repeating to Masae, as much for his own benefit, she felt, as hers, "the faster we go home. Next April, that's the goal. Maybe June. No longer than that." He worked late most nights in the Japanese tradition, flagging a bicycle-ricksha in town to bring him home over the long dirt road in the moonlight.

Each night Masae watched for her husband from the nursery window as she sang their daughter, Hiroko, to sleep. Hiroko, two years and nine months come the end of summer, was already developing her own idiosyncrasies. She fell asleep in one position only: curled up on her left side, right arm slung over the right half of her tiny bean-stuffed pillow, head burrowed under its left half. Masae didn't see how she could breathe, but she knew better than to tug away the pillow even if Hiroko was asleep.

Tonight, cranking open the window to feel the night breeze, Masae drew in a deep breath. With the climate so dry, the air had no real smell other than that of the dusty wooden sill over which she leaned. But Masae loved that instant when her face, dulled from the heat of day, first came into contact with the night air. She savored it so fully that if the cool breeze were a feather brushing her cheek, she could have counted its strands.

Two months ago, after the first enemy prisoners passed by, Masae had kept all the windows locked. Since then her vigilance had waned, but only slightly—enough to open a window, but not to leave it unattended. Even Koonyan, their heavyset maid who came two afternoons a week, still unnerved her; the girl never spoke, merely taking in Masae's Japanese orders without any expression. Recently Masae dreamed that Koonyan turned toward her and revealed a face without features, as smooth and blank as a stone. She admitted this to Shoji, with a self-deprecating little laugh. "Nothing to be afraid of," he told her. "Hoh, behind that face she's busy thinking about her little pet birds!"

Shoji's wry comment referred to a company function two months ago, which they had attended shortly after the prisoner procession. It was a Western-style welcome dinner held in their honor, at someone's home in the main town. Masae was seated beside the company interpreter, an elderly Japanese man who had studied Chinese classics at Kyoto University. Shoji sat across the table from them, his chin partially obscured by a vase of thick-petaled indigenous flowers. Last year a prisoner had escaped, the interpreter told them with a lilting Kansai accent. This Chinese man had hidden in the dark on someone's tiled roof, lying flat as a gyoza skin while the Army searched for him in the streets; he might have gone free if not for the Army's German shepherds. "See," Masae told her husband across the flowers, "it pays to play it safe!"

"But they're not overly antagonistic toward us," the interpreter had reassured them, "compared to other occupied provinces I've seen. Tai-huen's been under one warlord or another for dynasties. Here their focus is on small things, pet birds, for example. Every household has a pet bird in a bamboo cage."

"Aaa, well, they're peasants," Shoji said benevolently. He had studied global geological theory at Tokyo University, which held as much prestige as the interpreter's alma mater, and he was proud of his large-scale understanding of things.

"True, but it's not just that, I think. Sometimes the small focus is necessary. I myself find it crucial."

"Yes—no doubt." Shoji shot Masae a quick glance of confoundment over the flowers. It occurred to her that these fleshy petals might be indirectly related to a cactus species.

"Yes, it's crucial." A quality of sorrow in the interpreter's voice, deeper somehow than mere sympathy for the Chinese, threaded its way to Masae's sensibility through the muted clinks of silverware around her. "The immensity of this land . . ."

At her window now, looking out over the darkening plain for the jiggling light of Shoji's ricksha lantern, Masae let her thoughts drift out toward the Pun'An Desert. She had never seen a desert; she imagined it much like these plains except hotter and bleaker, stripped of its occasional oak trees and the comforting motion of rippling grass. An endless stretch of sand where men weakened, and died alone. Masae, being from Hiroshima, had grown up by an ocean that drowned thousands in storm seasons. Yet as a child she had sensed the water's expanse as full of promise—spreading out limitless before her, shifting, shimmering, like her future. She and her schoolmates had linked elbows and stood at the water's edge, digging their toes into the wet sand and singing out to sea at the tops of their voices: songs such as "Children of the Sea" or, if their mothers weren't around, the mountaineering song that Korean laborers sang, "Ali-lan." She remembered the tug of her heart when, on the way to school, she had followed with her eyes a white gull winging a straight line out to sea. But those were the impressions of youth. Masae was now at midlife, midpoint—Hiroko had been a late child—and for the first time she sensed the inevitability of moving from sea to desert.

The next night, for the third night in a row, Hiroko demanded that her mother read *Tomo-chan Plants Her Garden.* Masae sat on a floor cushion before the dark nursery window while Hiroko perched on her lap and turned the pages when told. Each page showed, with predictable monotony, yet another brightly colored fruit or vegetable ballooning up magically from its seed, hovering above it like the genie in their Arabian Nights book. They certainly looked nothing like the meager produce their maid brought home from the open-air market: desert vegetables, Masae thought. The big daikon radishes, for example. She was serving them raw, as all Japanese women did in the summer, finely grated and mounded on a blue plate to suggest the coolness of snow and water. But these radishes had no juicy crunch. They were as rubbery as boiled jellyfish and required rigorous chewing. Shoji didn't seem to notice—he was often exhausted when he came home—and lately Masae fancied that he was absorbing the radishes' essence. Since they had come to Tai-huen, something about him had shrunk in an indefinable way, as if an energy that once simmered right below the surface of his skin had retreated deep into his body.

Yet Shoji denied having any troubles, and laughed shortly at what a worrier she was. As long as Masae could remember,

Shoji's laughs had been too long—about two ha-ha's past the appropriate stopping point. They had always irritated her, those laughs, but lately Shoji stopped way before that point, as if to conserve them. She missed his long laughter now, the thoughtless abundance of it.

"The End," Masae concluded, slowly closing the book. Hiroko squirmed on her lap, and Masae could sense the wheels in her mind starting to turn, thinking up new questions about the story in order to postpone her bedtime. To deflect the questions, Masae picked Hiroko up and carried her to the window, upon which their faces were reflected in faint but minute detail, as if on the surface of a deep pool. The child's head gave off the warm scent of shampoo.

"Way out past those lights," she told her daughter, cranking open the window with her free hand, "is the desert, hora!" Their reflections twisted and vanished; coolness flowed in around them. A wild dog howled in the distance.

"What's a dizzert?"

"Lots of sand, nothing else. No people. No flowers."

"Ne, how come?" This, turning around to squint up at her mother.

"It's too dry for anything to grow."

Hiroko digested this in silence; then, "Are there rice balls?"

"No. There's nothing out there in the desert."

"What about milk?"

"No."

"What about"—she twisted in Masae's arms to peer back at the nursery—"toys?"

"*No.*"

"How come?"

Masae drew a deep breath. At such times she felt she was floundering in a churning river. She longed for Shoji—or any adult, for that matter—with whom she could follow a narrow stream of rational thought to some logical end.

"Mama told you why, remember?" she said. "You already know the answer. Yes, you do."

"The dizzert lost all its seeds!" Hiroko cried, tonight's story fresh in her mind. "You got to get some seeds. And then you can grow things." Masae agreed, and left the matter alone.

After Hiroko fell asleep, she returned to the window. The stars neither glimmered nor winked; they lay flat on the sky in shattered white nuggets. The town lights were yellower, a cozy cluster of them glowing in the distance with a stray gleam here and there. She imagined blowing the lights out with one puff, like candles.

Seeds. As a girl Masae had read a book on deserts, how it rained once every few years. After the rain, desert flowers burst into bloom only to die within two days, never seen by human eyes. Such short lives, ignorant of their terrible fate. She had wondered at the time how a seed could be trusted to stay alive in the sand; wouldn't it just dry up from years of waiting? In the driest, bleakest regions of the desert, who was checking whether flowers still bloomed at all? Aaa, Masae thought, this is what comes of keeping company with a child.

But one fact was indisputable; the Pun'An Desert was expanding. Shoji had mentioned it, only last night: spreading several centimeters each year, according to the latest scientific report. Killing the grass in its path like a conquering army. Wasn't it reasonable, then, that seeds *were* actually dying in this part of the world, leaving fewer and fewer of them to go around? An inexplicable sense of loss overwhelmed Masae. When Shoji's ricksha lantern bobbed into view, its light refracted through her tears and gleamed brighter than any evening star.

A prisoner procession was coming. Masae heard its faint *tan tan tantaka tan* from the living room, where she sat on the floor reading a letter from her mother. She had assumed, since that one procession in the beginning of summer, that prisoners would always come by after sunset. But it was still afternoon. Koonyan, the maid, was still here—her blank egg-shaped face had just peered in at her mistress as she glided silently down the hall—so it wasn't even five o'clock yet.

Masae was aware of the strange picture she must make to Koonyan, sitting in the middle of the floor while surrounded by perfectly good imported furniture. The company representative who arranged their move must have been an Anglophile; he had stocked the house with a modish array of brocaded ottomans and chaise longues, even the bench made of black iron out in the garden. The Nakazawas could not relax in such chairs. They installed tatami matting on the concrete floors, and Masae had Koonyan sew floor cushions for all the rooms. Shoji bought a saw and shortened the legs of the Western-style dining table so they could sit at ease during meals.

Don't you worry so much, her mother's letter said. Masae noted the slowness of the mail; the letter was dated August 10, 1942, more than four weeks ago. *We're all just fine. There've been only those two air raid alarms—not even a single hit. Rationing, though, has gotten much more inconvenient, and not having nice meals on the*

*table can be demoralizing, especially for your father! But I am confi-
dent in my heart that all this will have blown over by the time you sail
back. I can imagine how Hiro-chan will have grown . . .*

There was the heavy click of the back entrance doorknob
turning, then Hiroko's high-pitched voice: "Mama—Mama,
the festival's coming—" To Hiroko, who had experienced the
Koinobori Festival just before moving to China, drums always
meant festivals.

Masae followed her child as she ran toward the garden gate,
passing through the flickering shade of the pine tree. When
Hiroko got excited, her right arm always swung harder than
her left. The habit had started back in Hiroshima. She had been
carried about so often on the arm of one relative or another, her
left arm curled around the back of someone's neck, that when
she was set down she forgot to move her "neck" arm. "Mama, I
want to go!" Hiroko wailed without turning around. An image
flashed through Masae's mind of a man pouncing, catlike, from
the roof. But it faded. And she felt a sharp need to gaze at other
living faces, even Chinese ones. She turned to Koonyan, who
had followed her out, and nodded. Koonyan leaned a hefty
shoulder into the solid weight of the wood, face impassive
above her navy mandarin collar; Hiroko imitated her movements with self-important grimaces of effort. The rusty hinges
yielded with a prolonged creak.

About forty men, dressed in khaki uniforms, shuffled
toward them in three columns. Long shadows stretched out
behind them, narrow and wavery like floating seaweed. Herd-
ing the prisoners were four Japanese guards with German shepherds at their heels, dogs as tall as Hiroko. *"Wan wan!"*
shrieked Hiroko in delight, mimicking dog barks and leaning

forward as far as Masae's grip on her hand would allow. *"Wan wan!"* The dogs' ears—huge black-tipped triangles of fur—flicked to attention, but otherwise the German shepherds ignored her, stalking past with the controlled intensity of wolves. One Japanese guard, noticing Masae's kimono, gave a curt nod; she acknowledged it with a slight bow. The Chinese stared ahead, their brown faces blurred with exhaustion and the dust of the plains.

Tan tan tantaka tan, tan tan tantaka tan, beat the little drum at the head of the line. Hiroko, eyes crinkled up with joy, let out a loud excited squeal. She began dancing: standing in place, bending and straightening her knees in jerks that didn't quite match the drum's rhythm. Her ponytail flopped limply on the top of her head.

One tall prisoner about Shoji's age looked over at Hiroko, bright-eyed in her red sundress. The corners of his mouth stretched out in a reluctant smile. One by one the others began to grin, and Masae had a jumbled impression of teeth: stained teeth, buck teeth, missing teeth. The prisoners turned their heads and kept looking at the dancing child as they passed by, wrists bound behind them with strips of cloth; Hiroko beamed back, thrilled by the attention of all those adults.

And as the columns of men grew small in the distance, Masae felt this moment shrink into memory, shriveling and gathering into a small hot point in her chest: a stray seed. It could have so easily been lost. Hiroko would not remember this, nor would the dead prisoners. *The immensity of this land . . .* Ancient land, stretching out to desert beneath the blank blue sky of late summer.

Since My House
Burned Down

THEY ARE BURNING leaves at Koh-Dai Temple. The monks do it constantly this time of year, in late afternoon, when there is the least amount of wind. From upstairs, above the slate-tiled roofs of neighborhood houses, I watch the smoke unravel above branches of red maple. Even from four alleys away it reaches me through the closed glass window: pungent, like incense; reminiscent of some lost memory. Impending recognition rushes through my head like the feeling right before a sneeze, then is gone.

They say that snakes are sensitive to smell. Some species can sense their prey from a distance of several kilometers. This seems significant because when I was born, seventy-six years ago, it was in the year of the snake. Although I've lost much of my hearing, as well as a steadiness of hand and jaw, my connection to smell has deepened with age. It's not that I'm able to smell better but that I have stronger physical reactions to it: sometimes a tightening of the throat, a bittersweet stab in the breast, a queer sinking in my belly. My convictions have always been instinctive rather than logical. "Snake year people," my mother used to say, "lie close to the ground. They feel the earth's forces right up against their stomachs."

Stomachs. Yuri, my daughter-in-law, must be cooking dinner downstairs. For a split second, I thought I detected the metallic whiff of American tomato sauce, which always makes me feel vaguely threatened. I sniff again, but it's gone.

I knew nothing about tomato sauces until a restaurant in the Shin-Omiya district first introduced the Western omelette on its lunch menu. That was a long time ago, years before the war. I remember my daughter, Momoko, fourteen at the time, begging permission to go with her friends.

"But Momo-chan," I said to her, "I make you omelettes every morning."

My daughter gave me a pained look. "Mother, Western eggs are *completely* different!" They use no sugar, Momoko said; no fish base to mellow the flavor, no soy sauce for dipping. Her classmate's father had described them as salty. They were spiced with grated black peppercorns and spread with a thick acidic paste made from tinned tomatoes.

"Ara maa! How revolting," I said. "But go if you must." The problem of not knowing how to use silverware did not cross our minds till later. That was where Yuri came in. My daughter-in-law, Yuri, who at this moment is downstairs cooking something which I pray is Japanese cuisine. I haven't caught any other smells yet, so what struck me as tomato sauce may have been a fluke.

Back then Yuri had been a new bride in our home for only a few months. She was raised in Kobe, a cosmopolitan port city well known for its foreign restaurants and boutiques. Yuri's family was very modish, and very rich; her trousseau included, among the traditional silk kimonos, a twelve-piece set of blue-and-white English china and several knee-length dresses from France. One dress was sleeveless and black; all along its hem hung long tassellike fringes. Yuri said it was a tango dancing dress.

Naturally I had reservations about this bride. I hope, I told her with polite concern, that this city has enough culture to appreciate your taste in foreign clothes. I doubt if Yuri caught the sarcasm. Our city of Kyoto was Japan's capital for centuries, the birthplace of *The Tale of Genji,* the focal point of the ancient arts. We are far inland, strategically cloistered by lush green hills on three sides. These hills, in addition to the Kamo River—I offered this last fact on a more genial note—provided a year-round cocoon of moisture which gave Kyoto women the finest complexions in the country.

But my reservations went deeper. Yuri being born in a horse year had bothered me even before the marriage. It wasn't just me. Our extended family did a double take when they learned that my son, a rabbit year, was considering marriage to a horse. No doubt neighbors gossiped in the privacy of their homes; the dynamics of such a union were only too obvious. How could a timid rabbit (a male rabbit—the shame of it) control a headstrong steed? In the end, however, we all decided in favor of the match because Yuri came from such a decent—and wealthy—family.

When I was a child, a horse scroll hung in the tokonoma alcove of our guest room. It was ancient, originally painted in the Chinese royal court, and presented to my family by a city dignitary on the day of my great-grandfather's birth. If females born in horse years were to be pitied, then males born in horse years were cause for celebration and gifts. The stallion was painted on white parchment using no more than ten or twelve brushstrokes. The strokes throbbed with contained energy: the haunch a heavy, swollen curve of black ink; the tail a drag of half-dried, fraying bristles that created the effect of individual hairs swishing in space. The stallion's neck, lumpy with muscle, was caught in midturn. One large black nostril flared above bared teeth. What I remember sensing about this horse, captured by the artist in the split second before it bolted, was its imperviousness to anything other than its own alarm. That black eyeball, rolling back, would not see a small child like me underfoot. Its hooves would not feel what they crushed. That thick neck would not respond to reins.

I thought of that horse as I watched Yuri teach my Momoko how to use silverware. She looked very unlike my daughter, who had the classic Minamoto features: long, oval face, eyes slanting up like delicate brushstrokes. Yuri had a wide face; bold, direct eyes instead of dreamy ones; intense laughs like yelps. She was all smiles, eager to please. But some indefinable tension in her vitality reminded me of that horse. Something about her neck, too, although it wasn't thick or muscular (but then, any neck could look slender under that enormous face!).

Yes, there was inflexibility in that neck, noticeable when she inclined her head sideways in thanks or in acknowledgment, that robbed the gesture of a certain soft elegance.

Momoko was thrilled that Yuri's Kobe upbringing had included dining in Western-style restaurants. "Aaa, Yuri-san, you've saved me from becoming a *laughingstock*!" she breathed in that exaggerated way of teenagers. "I would have made some horrible mistake, not knowing any better, and shamed my whole *family*." At that moment, I wanted to slap my daughter. And Yuri too. Momoko's innocent words could not have cut me any deeper. We Minamotos were one of the five oldest samurai families in the Kansai region; Yuri's family crest came nowhere near ours in distinction. Since girlhood Momoko had been trained, as I once had, in every conceivable form of etiquette befitting her heritage: classical dance, stringed koto, tea ceremony, flower arranging, correct degrees of bowing for each social situation. She had nothing to be ashamed of. As if eating with outlandish foreign utensils even counted as manners!

Yuri had cooked up a traditional Japanese egg loaf for Momoko that night, since I kept no peppercorns or acidic tomato sauces in *my* kitchen, and served it at the low dining room table. Forks and knives glistened among her English china with the malevolence of surgical instruments. I sat quietly behind them on a floor cushion in the corner, sewing and watching this woman teach my child social behaviors I knew nothing about. Momoko's clumsy attempts made the metal utensils clang alarmingly against her plate.

"Place your forefinger here, like this," said Yuri, standing behind her and leaning over her shoulder to demonstrate. "That'll give you more leverage. Otherwise that fork'll slip right out of your hands." Momoko giggled and made a little bow of apology over her plate.

What a barbaric way to eat, I thought. Wielding iron spears and knives right at the table, stabbing and slicing—chores that should be performed in the privacy of a kitchen, leaving diners' energies free for thoughts of a higher order. At that moment a strange foreboding rose up through my belly: a sense that my world, indeed my entire understanding of it, was on the threshold of great change. I felt my fingers tremble over the sewing.

"Momoko," I called out from my corner, "Momoko. Sit up straight."

I have carried with me to this day the image of Momoko begging permission to go to the restaurant: a slender girl in an autumn kimono the exact shade of those maple leaves down by the temple. She stands beside a tree whose bark is sodden black from the heavy rain. Moss creeps up its trunk, and her fine white Minamoto complexion is a luminous contrast to the bitter autumn hues of black and green and rust. The poignance of the picture strikes me now as it did not then: that fine play of color, worthy of a Hiroshige etching, youth blooming in a season of endings. Momoko was to contract pneumonia that winter, and die months later.

My instincts were right.

There was the war, for one thing, the magnitude of which none of us could have predicted. Its hardships need not be discussed. We tacitly understand this, those of us who have survived: our longtime neighbors, my rabbit year son, even Yuri, who, as I always suspected, is 100 percent horse. "Remember that crazy old Uehara-san?" I occasionally say, laughing, to our old neighbor Mrs. Nakano in the alley. "How he missed his sushi so much, he used raw chicken instead of fish?"

"It didn't taste so bad, ne . . . ," she always says, and we both chuckle, as if looking back on happy times. We go no further. We never discuss the bombings.

Mr. Uehara was lucky; at least he owned chickens, living out in the country. He was our contact for black market rice, at a time when wartime currency was useless. I hate to think what that rice cost our family: bolts of fine watered silk, priceless porcelain vases handed down for generations since the Tokugawa Period.

We neighborhood women took the train into the countryside, since our men were either fighting abroad or, like my own husband, reported dead. Our train bumped leisurely through the crowded westside weaving district on its way out to flat farm fields, past narrow doorways of slatted wood and somber shrinelike roofs. In prosperous times one could have leaned out the train window and heard the deafening clatter of looms— *gat-tan-gat-tan*—coming from each house. Now, silence save for the occasional screech of ragged boys playing swords with long bamboo poles.

For the physical task of carrying, we wore navy blue *mompe* of the peasant class—I always think of them when I see today's popular pajamas. On the way there, we lugged our family treasures concealed in large *furoshiki* wraps. By the end of the day, the contents would be replaced by half a sack of rice and no more; we had all been warned about women who developed hernias from too much heavy lifting. At the farm, old Mr.

Uehara treated us to his startling lunch menus of raw chicken sushi. On one occasion, he served grasshoppers crisped over a fire and crumbled into brown flakes—these looked identical to the shaved bonito flakes we had eaten with our rice before the war; the texture, too, was identical, and with soy sauce the difference in taste was barely discernible. "Plenty of nutrients," Mr. Uehara told us with a sparkle in his eye. "In times of trouble, we must all use our heads." It was hard to say whether that sparkle came from his own good health or from the anticipation of receiving yet another installment of our family fortunes.

The loneliest time was afterwards on the platform, sitting on our sacks of rice and waiting for the whistle of the train. We had no energy left for small talk, and each of us sank down into her private gloom. By now, no doubt, Japan Railways has replaced that wooden platform with a concrete one, complete with an automatic ticket vending machine, but back then it was rickety, its planks weathered gray by the seasons. Orioles' nests swung from the exposed rafters on the roof, which rose high above the surrounding fields, throwing down its long shadows. Whenever a breeze swept over the long suzuki grasses, those black shadows quavered like reflections on a rippling sea. I had the sense of being marooned while the sun set on the end of the world.

I tried not to think of my husband, lying in some unmarked grave on Iwo Jima. I tried not to think of Momoko, dead these five years. But in such weak moments misery gathered in my breast so thick and clotted that it choked my breathing. The sound of crows cawing on their lonely flight home was unbearable.

At one point during those trips, I heard the music of the

fields. It wasn't so significant at the time. But some random memories, like my image of Momoko, are like that. Over time, they acquire a patina the way pearls gather luster. The sound I heard, a hushed soughing, brought to mind countless blades of grass rustling together and the millions of tiny lives—insects and birds and rodents—feeding and sleeping and growing beneath their cover. The breeze, filtering through the grasses, dislodged the sounds so that they rose up and, wafting on currents of air, hummed and whispered all around. A Masahide poem I learned in childhood floated to mind: *Since my house burned down / I now own a better view / of the rising moon.*

Peacetime ushered in what I think of as Yuri's era. Children became versed in silverware usage, as the Americans instituted hot lunch programs in the decimated schools. Knee-length cotton dresses, too, became common. Yuri dragged out her French trousseau dresses—practical-minded Mr. Uehara hadn't wanted those—and paraded through the open-air market among rows of chives and lotus roots, gaudy and unashamed in her moth-eaten silk. It was all terribly embarrassing.

Yet for the first time I desired her friendship. We had gone through a terrible war together—known so much loss—and like it or not, she was now part of my life: someone who remembered our old quality of living, our family's stature. I was a bit cowed, as well, by this harsh postwar energy sweeping the city: children marching through our alleys wearing Western school uniforms of navy and white, garish billboards with English words (which Yuri had learned to read back in Kobe, and was now teaching my son). But as I said, this was now

Yuri's era. She had no interest in friendship; the horse was already running with the bit between its teeth.

"Mother-san, I'll finish up here," she often said brightly as we were cooking together in the kitchen. This, before I had barely even finished washing the rice! I had to fight back just to stay standing.

"A! a! that's not necessary," I would reply. "I'm happy to do it. Why don't you just go relax, put on some cosmetics for when your husband comes home." Do *something,* so I can have grandchildren.

"I'm already wearing cosmetics." That short laugh of hers, like a yelp.

Our struggle progressed over the years until Yuri stopped playing fair. Her ultimate victory, driving me out of my own kitchen, finally arrived last year. To my credit, at least, it took several decades in coming. It was Toshihide, my own son, who delivered the blow to me in the garden, stepping cautiously across the moss to where I was bending over to feed the turtle in the stone vat. "Yuri has noticed," he said slowly and loudly into my ear, "that more than once . . . left on . . . gas on the stove. More than . . . refrigerator . . . closed all the way. Per-haps . . . old age. . . . Would you mind . . ." From the corner of my eye I saw Toshihide's Adam's apple shifting about like the nose of a rabbit. Aaa, I should have had another son! Momoko should have lived.

My whole life has been a process of losing security. Or iden-tity. Perhaps they are the same thing. I may not be a true snake. For each skin I have shed, there has been no new replacement.

I sit upstairs now, relieved of all my household duties, and look down at the smoke rising from Koh-Dai Temple. I wonder if the monks there contemplate life's cycle as they tend the fire, or if their mundane task is simply a welcome break from more serious duties. Leaves and twigs and straw, all leaving behind their inherent forms and evaporating into space. Next spring their ashes will reemerge without a trace of their former characteristics: as moss, as an earthworm, as a cherry tree whose fruit will be eaten by children in summer then converted to human matter. A pitiless world, this: refusing you the slightest sense of self to cling to.

It is two weeks later when I go for a stroll down to the Kamo River, which is three blocks from home in the opposite direction of the temple. I shuffle through the dappled shade of maple trees and hear cicadas shrilling *meeeeee* overhead, which is impossible in November; a combination, no doubt, of ingrained memory and the hearing aid I wear on my walks in case I meet someone I know.

I head toward a sunny bench overlooking the water. These days walking exhausts me. The river flows past, sunlight glinting on its surface like bright bees swarming over a hive. I can actually hear the bees buzzing, so I take out my hearing aid and put it in my handbag. I sun myself like this for a long time, eyes half shut. I conjure up from memory the surface sounds of the river, its tiny slurps and licks as countless currents tumble over one another. I remember too the soft roar in flood time of the undercurrent as it drags silt and pebbles out to sea.

The music comforts me. I imagine dissolving into the

water, being borne along on its current. Something slowly unclenches within my chest. I am pared down, I think suddenly, to Masahide's poem. And I sense with a slow-mounting joy how wide this river is, and how very deep, with its waters rolling out toward an even vaster sea; and the quiet surge of my happiness fills my chest to bursting.

Shibusa

"YOU HAVE A sensibility for elegant manners," my tea ceremony teacher once told me, "the way a musician has an ear for pitch." Even before I could read, mothers were pointing out my floor bows as examples to their daughters: spine straight, its line barely breaking even when my head approached the floor; rear end clamped to heels the entire time with tensed quadriceps. As a teenager I performed the "admiration of vessel" step at tea ceremonies with an artistry beyond my years. I held out the ceramic bowl before me with arms neither straight nor bent, but rounded in a pleasing curve. Tilting my head just so, rotating the bowl in my hands the requisite three times, I lost myself in the countless subtle ways glaze changes color when shot through with sunlight.

Such rituals of etiquette lifted me to an aesthetic plane, where often I had the sense—though I could not have articulated it then—of life being a dance, to be performed with stately grace.

But my bearing lacked that ultimate essence of refinement, described by elders as *shibusa*. It had to do with something more than mere maturity and was hard to define. The Buddha's smile of sorrowful sentience had this quality. A maple leaf in autumn, slowly twisting during its long fall to earth, evoked *shibusa;* that same leaf in midsummer, growing healthy and green from its branch, did not. "Aaa, it will come—" I remember my teacher saying with a sigh.

As a young bride, I was besotted with my husband, Yukio. He was square of face, with a firm straight line of a mouth and hair slicked back from his brow with immaculate comb lines. More than once, others commented on his likeness to those fine three-quarter profiles of samurai painted on New Year's kites. Like a samurai, Yukio was well versed in martial arts—fifteen years of kendo training—and displayed, unconsciously, those fluid transitions of movement so prized in Noh theater. He was successful in business as well: a fast-rising executive at Kokusai Kogyo, an import-export conglomerate. Years later this company would be disbanded in the aftermath of our military defeat, but at the time it had the clout and prestige of today's Mitsubishi.

Early in our marriage Yukio was transferred overseas, to the Chinese province of Pei-L'an. It was 1937, seven months after the province had fallen to Japanese rule. "Don't forget to write!" my girlfriends clamored; then, in hushed tones, "And give us details! Those women's bound feet . . ."

One would think that sailing away to China would have exposed me to the cruelties of life. Today there is fervent talk on the radio of our soldiers' atrocities there: villages burned, women raped, soldiers butchered in prison camps. But all I knew of Pei-L'an province was our executives' housing compound: nineteen eaves sweeping up, pagoda-style, their ceramic roof shingles glazed a deep Prussian blue. The high wall enclosing our compound was white stucco, and the large main gate (through which we women passed only when escorted by our husbands) was topped with a miniature stylized roof in matching blue tile. I had little curiosity about how the region beyond had been defeated, and it would have been ungallant, ill-bred even, for Yukio to disclose the morbid details of war to a young bride. I wonder now how much he, as a mere civilian, knew of all this at the time. At any rate, I was more interested in immediate events, like the ripening of persimmons in autumn. That fine play of color—bright orange globes against the dark blue—gave me stabs of delight; it added an exotic touch to this new foreign experience.

The company had hired nineteen housemaids from the local village—one for each house. They arrived each day at dawn and were let in by the compound guards. Sometimes Yukio and I, drowsing under our futon, heard their faint voices coming up the main path, the harsh grating of consonants making the women sound as if they were perpetually quarreling.

Xi-Dou, the maid assigned to our home, was about my age. I sneaked curious looks at her while she worked; back home, domestic servants were rare. Her feet, far from being bound, were even bigger than mine. But despite her callused hands and faded mandarin tunic, she had a pleasing face, with full lips and wide-set eyes. She never laughed and only rarely smiled—wistfully, with a slight pucker of brows. Those smiles caused me intense guilt over my own newlywed bliss, which seemed selfish and indulgent in contrast. "Yukio," I said one night when we were lying in bed gazing up at the shadowed beams of the ceiling, "I wish Xi-Dou could join us for dinner."

I heard the slow crunch of his buckwheat-husk pillow as he turned his head in my direction. "Xi-Dou? The maid?"

"I saw the poor thing crouching on a stool in the kitchen," I said, "eating our leftovers. It ruins the harmony of this home for me, seeing something like that."

"Maa, such a gentle heart you have . . . ," Yukio murmured, his forefinger along my cheek as slow and deft as the rest of his movements. "And a face to match. . . . But"—his finger trailed away—"that's the procedure with servants. I assure you she doesn't take it personally. The food here is a lot better than what she's getting at home."

"It seems impolite, when she's already right here in the house," I said.

Yukio propped himself up on his elbow, looking down at me with his handsome samurai face. "Darling?" he said; in the moonlight his brows lifted in amusement like dark wings. "We just defeated these people in a *war*."

I did not reply.

"I'm not suggesting," Yukio said finally, "that etiquette—or consideration, whatever—shouldn't exist in wartime. Far from it. People need it to cope with life. But your nebulous gesture isn't practical. Ne? It would give her false hopes, make her life look bleaker in contrast."

"Wouldn't it give her—dignity? Or—" My voice trailed off

in embarrassment. He was right, I saw that now; what would Xi-Dou want with the company of Japanese strangers?

"True kindness, in my opinion," said Yukio, "is good pay." He kissed my forehead once, twice, then fell back on his pillow with a scrunch. "Give her occasional tips, how about that? It'll do you both good." In a moment I heard his soft snore.

I was not fully satisfied by Yukio's solution. On the one hand it pleased my sense of order: for each situation, there should be a proper and logical course of action. Yet some additional dimension was missing, though I could not have defined it.

His comment interested me: *people need it to cope with life.* That had not been my own experience. I had never used etiquette to "cope." But I understood how its ethereal quality, like temple incense, might lift one out from the realm of daily cares.

I continued gazing up at the ceiling. These Chinese roofs were lower than I was used to, pressing down upon me in the darkness. Maa—I thought—whether in kendo or in matters of judgment, Yukio always hits the heart of a matter with one sure blow.

Yukio soon became friends with another executive in our compound, Mr. Nishitani. They were the only two men in management who were still in their thirties. Both were tall and striking, with that genial assurance that comes from a lifetime of excellent schooling and privileged treatment. Nishitani-san, a bachelor, began dining frequently at our house.

In certain ways Nishitani-san was the opposite of my husband. With Yukio one got the impression that behind each word or motion was a hidden reserve of strength, of discipline. It was evident in the way he told jokes at company parties: so deadpan that when he delivered his punch line it took a moment for his audience to react. Only after they burst into laughter, roaring and shrieking, did Yukio give in to laughter himself, his rich baritone notes pealing forth from well-conditioned lungs.

Nishitani-san, by contrast, carried all his energy on the surface. His smiles were dazzling, sudden and unexpected like flashes of sunlight on water; the older wives whispered among themselves that those smiles took your breath away, quite! Somebody once said that even the air around Nishitani-san seemed to shimmer. In excitement his voice rose and his cowlick shot up like a tuft of grass; in a burst of good humor he was not above breaking into some Kabuki chant—right in public—or improvising a silly jig. "Won't you ever learn to behave—" I chided him with motherly resignation, though I was five years younger than he. Compared to Yukio, Nishitani-san was just a bit boyish for my taste. But that quality would later endear him to my little boy, Kin-chan, with whom I had recently learned I was pregnant.

Xi-Dou, our maid, fancied Nishitani-san. On the evenings he came over she plaited her hair loosely, draping it over one shoulder in a long gleaming braid instead of pinning it up into a bun. On a few occasions I could have sworn her lips were faintly stained with lipstick. One of mine? I wondered. I never mentioned this to Yukio, but it did occur to me, once or twice, that "coping with life" was not such a clear-cut business as he had implied. Certain needs, however impractical, will transcend all others. From the corner of my eye I watched Xi-Dou as she backed away from our table, clutching the empty serving tray to her chest, then turned to the door with one last look over her shoulder at Nishitani-san. As far as I could tell, he was oblivious to her presence.

Nishitani-san brought out a side of Yukio that I did not often see. When it was just the two of us, my husband was reverently tender or else serious and philosophical. But when Nishitani-san came to dinner he became witty, full of one amusing anecdote after another. Nishitani-san, who flushed easily when drinking sake, responded in kind, determined not to be outdone. I would laugh and laugh, gasping for breath, forgetting even to cover my mouth with my hand, till the muscles in my cheeks ached.

Those were such happy times, right before the Second World War.

Sometimes I left them—either to give Xi-Dou instructions or else to use the bathroom, something I did frequently now that I was expecting. I was not yet far enough along to feel the baby inside me, but surely it was soaking up all this laughter, growing stronger and finer as a result. In the privacy of the hallway I often stopped to tuck in wisps of hair which, on such evenings, invariably came loose from my chignon. Before me was a small window with a view of the Xiang-Ho mountains. Beyond the pagoda-style roofs I could make out their blue outline in the gathering dusk, high and jagged in the distance. And I, heartbeat still high from the hilarity of the evening, would stand in the hallway and gaze out for a while before going on my way. I thought of Yukio's deep laughter, of his large hands; of this coming child and of business continuing to boom—and I forced myself to be calm, to concentrate on those somber mountains darkening and fading beyond the compound walls that enclosed us.

From the next room I could hear the men's deep voices, laughing.

I have learned since that no experience lives on in memory. Not in the true sense. It becomes altered, necessarily, by subsequent events. My memory of China is steeped in a sense of encroaching doom that was surely not present then, like a scene flooded with the last rays of sunset.

War was declared in 1941, when Kin-chan was three years old. Kokusai Kogyo pulled up its Pei-L'an branch, and we employees sailed back in shifts to our various homes in Japan. Nishitani-san sailed home to some town near Nagasaki; the three of us came home to Ueno. Bombs dropped on our city; there were fires. One day, while I was standing in a rationing line on the other side of town, a bomb dropped on our neighborhood. What terrible luck that Yukio was home on leave that week; I had left him and Kin-chan in the garden, playing hide-and-seek. Our son was five years old.

Over the decades, this period has faded in my memory. Only occasionally now will it seep out into my body, staining my saliva with a faint coppery taste, which makes me think that somewhere, within the tissues and nerves of my body, I am bleeding.

One morning a year after the surrender—Kin-chan would have turned eight by now—an odd thing happened.

I was crouched beside the kitchen door out in the alley, watering my potted chrysanthemums. In one hand, I held the watering can; with the other, I was twisting off a browned leaf here and there. Hearing the slow *k'sha k'sha* of gravel, I turned around to see a seafood peddler pass me in the alley, bowed under the yoke of his pannier. His blue jacket looked unfamiliar; he was not from our neighborhood.

This was not unusual; residents of other areas often used our alley as a shortcut to Kamogawa Bridge on their way downtown.

As the man bowed slightly, in gratitude and apology for using this shortcut, our eyes met briefly. Then he stopped, a startled look on his face. He lowered his baskets, brimming with shijimi shells and pickled seaweed, onto the gravel before me. Something about him looked familiar—perhaps the shape of his lips, curled up slightly at the ends as if to get a jump start on a smile. But I could not place him.

The peddler stepped toward me, then bowed deeply. It was a well-trained bow, slow and straight-backed, unsettling in a man of his station. I hurriedly rose, still holding my watering can. "Goto-san, do you remember me?" he said. "I'm Nishitani. I once had the pleasure of your friendship, and your husband's, back in Pei-L'an."

Again our eyes met, and I glanced away. The shame in his look made my heart contract with pain. Even for such times, this was extreme misfortune. I fancied I could feel his loss of face pulsing out toward me, like heat waves.

We exchanged pleasantries. Nishitani-san had lines on either side of his mouth, like parentheses. Had they been there before? Something seemed different about his features—he had lost that shimmer, I think now, which had once played upon them.

"Nishitani-san, do you have a moment to sit down?" I sank down onto the kitchen step. "Here with me?" My voice came from far away. Even the weather had a surreal quality to it, I remember. It was overcast. The sky was not gray but whitish, like thick membrane, and light glowed behind it with a brightness almost brutal.

"Saa, that would be fine," he said. A faint version of his old smile brought back China to me, like a whiff of old scent. "Just for a few minutes."

Nishitani-san offered no explanation of his situation, nor did he mention what he was doing in this part of the country. I avoided looking in the direction of his baskets, for I wanted to spare him as much discomfort as possible; I kept my gaze trained on his face and never once glanced down at the hip-length vendor jacket he wore, cobalt blue with the store owner's name written in white brushstrokes down the length of its collar. Nishitani-san smelled so strongly of fish blood, sitting beside me, that my temples were tightening into a headache. And he had once used such lovely cologne, from Paris.

He asked after Yukio and Kin-chan, and I told him, in the briefest terms. "Aaa, here too . . . ," he murmured. I remembered then that he had lived near Nagasaki. "How you must have suffered," he said after a silence, gazing at my face. I knew he was registering the premature streaks of white in my hair, the sun damage on my once flawless complexion.

"Do you remember," Nishitani-san said abruptly, and he began to reminisce about the delicious roast duck at our dinners, Yukio's old jokes, the comical quirks of our compound neighbors. I heard in his voice a new gravity, a new tenderness, that seemed to lift each memory—like some precious jewel—and hold it up in wonderment to the light.

"You know," I said, "Kin-chan missed you for almost a month after we sailed home. 'Uncle *Nee*-tani,' he kept saying with that lisp of his, and he looked so worried, with his little forehead all wrinkled up, that everybody just had to *laugh*—"

"A whole month, really?" Nishitani-san said. His lips curved up into his old dazzling smile. "That was unusually long for a three-year-old!"

"You see, hora, you're the type," I said with my old playful air, "who makes a huge impression on everyone he meets!" I froze then at my choice of words, for it skirted a little too close to the impression he would be leaving me with today. But Nishitani-san seemed not to mind, for he tipped back his head and laughed.

I pictured him back in China, on a sunny Sunday afternoon a few months before war was declared. He had been striding away after luncheon at our home, a tall, confident man; the force of his gait made the back of his white shirt, always immaculately starched, balloon out above his belt like a full sail. "Uncle *Nee*-tani! Uncle *Nee*-tani!" Kin-chan had shrieked, running after him through the dappled light beneath the persimmon trees, losing his red sandal in the dirt, fumbling to put it back on, then losing it again after a few steps.

Nishitani-san had glanced back. "Escape, Nishitani-san, escape!" I called out to him, laughing and shooing him away with both hands. He had flashed me a big white smile and, with a boyish laugh, trotted away in mock haste, leaving Kin-chan bawling in the middle of the path.

Remembering all this, I felt the prickle of approaching tears and lowered my eyes to hide it. Nishitani-san was still laughing; it surprised me that his hands, red and raw like a laborer's, were trembling on his knees.

"The aristocrats of the ancient court," I say, "were devout Buddhists." It is decades later, and I am lecturing to my older tea ceremony students on the origins of etiquette.

"Buddha taught that life is filled with pain," I tell them. And suddenly an image of Nishitani-san's hands comes to mind, as they looked one day in the year 1946. There were dark scabs on his knuckles, hard as horn and soon to become calluses; on the rest of his hands were thin red scratches. I remembered my first glimpse of his baskets, full to the brim despite the lateness of the morning hour.

Clearly he was new to this, and struggling; he had not yet perfected that peculiar air vendors have, the bland unthinking cheerfulness which attracts customers.

"Filled with pain," I say to my students, "and sorrow."

"Hai, Teacher," the girls murmur in their high-pitched voices.

On that long-ago morning I pulled out my coin purse from my apron pocket—my hands, too, were trembling now—but before I could speak, Nishitani-san shook his head no. It was quick, a mere jerk—the imperceptible warning one gives in the presence of a third party. I slipped the purse back in my pocket.

"Those aristocrats, influenced by Buddha's teachings," I tell my students, "felt that nobility of spirit was the grace—or ability—to move through this world voluntarily, as a game or dance. And they passed down their ideal through the rituals of etiquette, ne? Polite speech, for example. Even today we refer to an honorable person not as having been killed, but as having condescended to play at dying."

The girls nod politely, blankly.

Today, what strikes me most about that morning—for memory will always shift focus—is our wordless farewell as Nishitani-san and I bowed to each other. It would be many years before I linked the essence of our bow with that of Kenryu's famous poem about a rice plant: *weighed down with grain / making graceful bows / in the wind.* How lovely our bows would have seemed to a casual onlooker: stately, seasoned, like movements in a sacred dance.

Aftermath

IN IMAMIYA PARK the boys are playing dodge-ball, a new American game. Their voices float indistinctly on the soft summer evening. Behind them tall poplars rise up through the low-lying dusk, intercepting the last of the sun's rays, which dazzle the leaves with white and gold.

Makiko can hardly believe her son, Toshi, belongs with these older boys. Seven years old! Once his growth had seemed commensurate with the passage of time. These last few years, however, with the war and surrender, the changes have come too fast, skimming her consciousness like skipped pebbles over water.

Makiko is grateful the war is over. But she cannot ignore a niggling sense that Japan's surrender has spawned a new threat more subtle, more diffuse. She can barely articulate it, even to herself; feels unmoored, buffeted among invisible forces that surge up all around her. Her son's thin body, as if caught up in these energies, is rapidly lengthening. Look! Within that circle in the dirt he is dodging, he is feinting; his body twists with an unfamiliar grace, foreshadowing that of a young man.

Toshi's growth is abetted by a new lunch program at school, subsidized by the American government, which has switched, with dizzying speed, from enemy to ally. Each day now, her son comes home with alien food in his stomach: bread, cheese, bottled milk. Last week, in the pocket of his shorts, Makiko found a cube of condensed peanut butter (an American dessert, Toshi explained) that he had meant to save for later. It was coated with lint from his pocket, which he brushed off, ignoring her plea to "get rid of that filthy thing."

Each day now, Toshi comes home with questions she cannot answer: Who was Magellan? How do you say "my name is Toshi" in English? How do you play baseball?

Makiko shows him the ball games her own mother taught her. She bounces an imaginary ball, chanting a ditty passed down from the Edo Period:

> *yellow topknots*
> *of the Portuguese wives*
>
> *spiraled like seashells*
> *and stuck atop their heads*
>
> *hold one up, to your ear*
> *shake it up and down*

> *one little shrunken brain*
> *is rattling inside*

In the old days, she tells him, they used to put something inside the rubber balls—maybe a scrap of iron, she wasn't sure—that made a rattling noise. Toshi, too old now for this sort of amusement, sighs with impatience.

Just four years ago, Toshi's head had been too big for his body—endearingly out of proportion, like the head of a stuffed animal. Even then he had a manly, square-jawed face, not unlike that of a certain city council candidate displayed on election posters at the time. "Mr. Magistrate," her husband, Yoshitsune, nicknamed the boy. Before he went off to war, Yoshitsune and their son had developed a little routine. "Oyi, Toshi! Are you a man?" Yoshitsune would prompt in his droll tone, using the word *otoko,* with its connotations of male bravery, strength, and honor. He asked this question several times a day, often before neighbors and friends.

"Hai, Father! I am a man!" little Toshi would cry, stiffening at soldierly attention as he had been coached, trembling with eagerness to please. His short legs, splayed out from the knees as if buckling under the weight of his head, were still dimpled with baby fat.

"Maaa! An excellent, manly answer!" the grown-ups praised, through peals of laughter.

Makiko had laughed too, a faint constriction in her throat, for recently Yoshitsune had remarked to her, "When I'm out fighting in the Pacific, that's how I'm going to remember him." After that she began watching their child closely, trying to memorize what Yoshitsune was memorizing. Later, when her husband was gone, it comforted her to think that the same images swam into both their minds at night. Even today, Toshi's three-year-old figure is vivid in her mind. On the other hand, she has not fully absorbed the war years, still shrinks from those memories and all that has followed.

Foreigners, for instance, are now a familiar sight. American Army jeeps with beefy red arms dangling out the windows roar down Kagane Boulevard, the main thoroughfare just east of Toshi's school. "Keep your young women indoors," the neighbors say. Makiko has watched an occasional soldier offering chocolates or peanuts to little children, squatting down to their level, holding out the treat—it seems to her they all have hairy arms—as if to a timid cat. Just yesterday Toshi came home, smiling broadly and carrying chocolates—not one square but three. Bile had surged up in Makiko's throat, and before she knew it, she had struck them right out of his hand and onto the kitchen floor. "How could you!" she choked as Toshi, stunned, burst into sobs. "How could you?! Your father, those men killed your *father*!"

This evening Makiko has come to the park with a small box of caramels, bought on the black market with some of the money she was hoarding to buy winter yarn. "In the future," she will tell him, "if you want something so badly, you come to me. Ne? Not to them."

On a bench in the toddlers' section, now deserted, she waits for her son to finish his game with the other boys. All the other mothers have gone home to cook dinner. The playground equipment has not been maintained since the beginning of the war. The swing set is peeling with rust; the free-standing animals—the ram, the pig, the rooster—rest on broken-down springs, and their carnival paint has washed away, exposing more rusted steel.

Ara maaa! Her Toshi has finally been hit! Makiko feels a mother's pang. He is crossing the line to the other side now, carrying the ball. Makiko notes the ease with which the fallen one seems to switch roles in this game, heaving the ball at his former teammates without the slightest trace of allegiance.

This year, Makiko is allowing Toshi to light the incense each evening before the family altar. He seems to enjoy prayer time much more now that he can use matches. She also regularly changes which photograph of her husband is displayed beside the miniature gong. This month's photograph shows Yoshi-tsune in a long cotton *yukata,* smoking under the ginkgo tree in the garden. Sometimes, in place of a photograph, she displays an old letter or one of his silk scent bags, still fragrant after a bit of massaging. The trick is to keep Toshi interested, to present his father in the light of constant renewal.

"Just talk to him inside your mind," she tells her son. "He wants to know what you're learning in school, what games you're playing. Just like any other father, ne? Don't leave him behind, don't ignore him, just because he's dead." She wonders if Toshi secretly considers his father a burden, making demands from the altar, like a cripple from a wheelchair.

"Your father's very handsome in this picture, ne?" she says tonight. Within the lacquered frame, her son's father glances up from lighting a cigarette, a bemused half smile on his face, as if he is waiting to make a wry comment.

Toshi nods absently. Frowning, he slashes at the matchbox

with the expert flourish of a second-grade boy. The match rips into flames.

"Answer properly! You're not a little baby anymore."

"Hai, Mother." Toshi sighs with a weary, accommodating air, squaring his shoulders in a semblance of respectful attention. Makiko remembers with sorrow the big head, the splayed legs of her baby boy.

It amazes her that Toshi has no memory of the routine he once performed with his father. "What *do* you remember of him?" she prods every so often, hoping to dislodge some new memory. But all that Toshi remembers of his father is being carried on one arm before a sunny window.

"Maaa, what a wonderful memory!" Makiko encourages him each time. "It must have been a very happy moment!"

When would this have taken place: which year, which month? Would even Yoshitsune have remembered it, this throwaway moment that, inexplicably, has outlasted all the others in their son's mind? She tries conjuring it up, as if the memory is her own. For some reason she imagines autumn, the season Yoshitsune sailed away: October 1942. How the afternoon sun would seep in through the nursery window, golden, almost amber, advancing with the slow, viscous quality of Tendai honey, overtaking sluggish dust motes and even sound. She wishes Toshi could remember the old view from that upstairs window: a sea of gray-tiled roofs drowsing in the autumn haze, as yet unravaged by the fires of war.

"I'm done," Toshi says.

"What! Already? Are you sure?"

"Hai, Mother." Already heading for the dining room, where supper lies waiting on the low table, he slides back the shoji door in such a hurry that it grates on its grooves. Makiko considers calling him back—his prayers are getting shorter and shorter—but the incident with the chocolates is still too recent for another reprimand.

She follows him into the dining room. "A man who forgets his past," she quotes as she scoops rice into his bowl, "stays at the level of an animal." Toshi meets her eyes with a guilty, resentful glance. "Go on," she says blandly, "eat it while it's hot."

Toshi falls to. In order to supplement their meager rice ration, Makiko continues to mix in chopped *kabura* radishes—which at least resemble rice in color—as she did during the war. Sometimes she switches to chopped turnips. At first, before the rationing became strict, Toshi would hunch over his rice bowl with his chopsticks, fastidiously picking out one bit of vegetable after another and discarding it onto another plate. Now, he eats with gusto. It cuts her, the things he has grown used to. As a grown man he will reminisce over all the wrong things, things that should never have been a part of his childhood: this shameful pauper food; blocks of peanut paste covered with lint; enemy soldiers amusing themselves by tossing chocolate and peanuts to children.

Later, Toshi ventures a question. Makiko has noticed that nighttime—the black emptiness outside, the hovering silence—still cows him a little, stripping him of his daytime cockiness. After his good-night bow, Toshi remains kneeling in bowing position on the tatami floor. He says, "I was thinking, Mama, about how I'm seven—and how I only remember things that happened after I was three. So that means I've forgotten a whole half of my life. Right?"

"That's right," Makiko says. He is looking up at her, his brows puckered in a look of doleful concentration that reminds her of his younger days. "But it's perfectly normal, Toshi-kun. It's to be expected."

He is still thinking. "So when I get older," he says, "am I going to keep on forgetting? Am I going to forget you, too?"

Makiko reaches out and strokes his prickly crew cut. "From this age on," she says, "you're going to remember everything, Toshi-kun. Nothing more will ever be lost."

In the middle of the night, Makiko awakes from a dream in which her husband, Yoshitsune, is hitting her with a fly-swatter. She lies paralyzed under her futon, outrage buzzing in her chest. Details from the dream wash back into her mind: Yoshitsune's smile, distant and amused; the insolent way he wielded the swatter, as if she were hardly worth the effort.

A blue sheet of moonlight slips in through the space between two sliding panels.

In the first year or two after Yoshitsune's death, this sort of thing would happen often, and not always in the form of dreams. There were times—but hardly ever anymore; why tonight?—when, in the middle of washing the dishes or sweeping the alley, some small injustice from her past, long forgotten, would rise up in Makiko's mind, blotting out all else till her heart beat hard and fast. Like that time, scarcely a month after their wedding, when Yoshitsune had run into his old girlfriend at Nanjin Station and made such a fuss: his absurd, rapt gaze; the intimate timbre of his voice as he inquired after her welfare.

And there was the time—the only time in their entire marriage—when Yoshitsune had grabbed Makiko by the shoulders and shaken her hard. He'd let go immediately, but not before she felt the anger in his powerful hands and her throat had choked up with fear. That, too, was early on in the marriage, before Makiko learned to tolerate his sending sizable sums of money home to his mother each month.

What is to be done with such memories?

They get scattered, left behind. Over these past few years, more pleasant recollections have taken the lead, informing all the rest, like a flock of birds, heading as one body along an altered course of nostalgia.

She has tried so hard to remain true to the past. But the weight of her need must have been too great: her need to be comforted, her need to provide a legacy for a small, fatherless boy. Tonight she senses how far beneath the surface her own past has sunk, its outline distorted by deceptively clear waters.

Toshi has been counting the days till Tanabata Day. A small festival is being held at the riverbank—the first one since the war. It will be a meager affair, of course, nothing like it used to be: no goldfish scooping, no soba noodles, no fancy fireworks. However, according to the housewives at the open-air market, there will be a limited number of sparklers (the nicest kind anyway, Makiko tells her son) and traditional corn grilled with soy sauce, which can be purchased out of each family's ration allowance.

Because of a recent after-dark incident near Kubota Temple involving an American soldier and a young girl, Makiko's younger brother has come by this evening to accompany them to the festival. Noboru is a second-year student at the local university.

"Ne, Big Sister! Are you ready yet?" he keeps calling from the living room. Makiko is inspecting Toshi's nails and the back of his collar.

"Big Sister," Noboru says, looking up as Makiko finally appears in the doorway, "your house is too immaculate, I get nervous every time I come here!" He is sitting stiffly on a floor cushion, sipping homemade persimmon tea.

"Well," Makiko answers, "I hate filth." She tugs down her knee-length dress. She has switched, like most women, to Western dresses—they require less fabric—but it makes her irritable, having to expose her bare calves in public.

"Aaa," says young Noboru from his floor cushion, "but I, for one, am fascinated by it. The idea of it, I mean. What's that old saying—'Nothing grows in a sterile pond'? Just think, Big Sister, of the things that come out of filth. A lotus, for example. Or a pearl. Just think: a pearl's nothing more than a grain of dirt covered up by oyster fluid! And life itself, Big Sister, billions of years ago—taking shape for the first time in the primordial muck!"

"Maa maa, Nobo-kun." She sighs, double-checking her handbag for coin purse, ration tickets, and handkerchief. "You seem to be learning some very interesting concepts at the university."

Toshi is waiting by the front door in shorts and a collared shirt, impatiently rolling the panel open and then shut, open and then shut.

Finally, they are on their way, strolling down the narrow

alley in the still, muggy evening. The setting sun angles down on the east side of the alley, casting a pink and orange glow on the charred wooden lattices where shadows reach, like long heads of snails, from the slightest of protrusions. In the shadowed side of the alley, one of the buck-toothed Yamada daughters ladles water from a bucket onto the asphalt around her door, pausing, with a good-evening bow, to let them pass. The water, colliding with warm asphalt, has burst into a smell of many layers: asphalt, earth, scorched wood, tangy dragon's beard moss over a mellower base of tree foliage; prayer incense and tatami straw, coming from the Yamadas' half-open door; and mixed in with it all, some scent far back from Makiko's own childhood that falls just short of definition.

"We Japanese," Noboru is saying, "must reinvent ourselves." There are, he tells her, many such discussions now at the university. "We must change to fit the modern world," he says. "We mustn't allow ourselves to remain an occupied nation." He talks of the new constitution, of the new trade agreements. Makiko has little knowledge of politics. She is amused—disquieted, too—by this academic young man, who before the war was a mere boy loping past her window with a butterfly net over his shoulder.

"Fundamental shifts . . . ," Noboru is saying, " . . . outdated pyramidal structures." Lately he has taken to wearing a hair pomade with an acrid metallic scent. It seems to suggest fervor, fundamental shifts.

"Toshi-kun!" Makiko calls. "Don't go too far." The boy stops running. He walks, taking each new step in exaggerated slow motion.

"So much change!" she says to Noboru as she tugs at her

cotton dress. "And so fast. Other countries had centuries to do it in."

"Soh soh, Big Sister!" Noboru says. "Soh soh. But we have no choice, that's a fact. You jettison from a sinking ship if you want to survive."

The pair approach Mr. Watanabe, watering his potted morning glories in the twilight. Holding his watering can in one hand, the old man gives them a genteel bow over his cane. "Yoshitsune-san," he murmurs politely, "Makiko-san." He then turns back to his morning glories, bending over them with the tenderness of a mother with a newborn.

"Poor Watanabe-san, ne," Noboru whispers. "He gets more and more confused every time we see him."

Yes, poor Mr. Watanabe, Makiko thinks. Bit by bit he is being pulled back in, like a slowing planet, toward some core, some necessary center of his past. Laden with memory, his mind will never catch up to Noboru's new constitution or those new trade agreements, or even the implications of that billboard with English letters—instructions for arriving soldiers?—rising above the blackened rooftops and blocking his view of the Tendai hills.

Oddly, Mr. Watanabe's mistake has triggered a memory from the past: Makiko is strolling with her husband this summer evening. For one heartbeat she experiences exactly how things used to be—that feel of commonplace existence, before later events imposed their nostalgia—with a stab of physical recognition, impossible to call up again. Then it is gone, like the gleam of a fish, having stirred up all the waters around her.

They walk on in silence. "Toshi-kun!" she calls out again.

"Slow down." Toshi pauses, waiting for them; he swings at the air with an imaginary bat. "Striku! Striku!" he hisses.

It occurs to Makiko that this war has suspended them for too long in an artificial, unsustainable state of solidarity. For a while, everyone had clung together in the bomb shelter off Nijiya Street, thinking the same thoughts, breathing in the same damp earth and the same warm, uneasy currents made by bodies at close range. But that is over now.

Makiko thinks of her future. She is not so old. She is still full of life and momentum. There is no doubt that she will pass through this period and on into whatever lies beyond it, but at a gradually slowing pace; a part of her, she knows, will lag behind in the honeyed light of prewar years.

"Toshi-kun!" she cries. "Wait!" Her son is racing ahead, his long shadow sweeping the sunlit fence as sparrows flutter up from charred palings.

At her first glimpse of the festival, Makiko's stomach sinks. Although she has come to this festival for Toshi's sake only— she herself having no interest in children's festivals, not having attended a Tanabata Night fair since her own teenage years— she is nonetheless taken unawares by the difference between the bright, colorful booths of her childhood and what now stands before her: four poles in the earth, supporting a crude black canopy made from some kind of industrial tarpaulin. A few tattered red paper lanterns, probably dug out from someone's attic, hang forlornly from the corners. Under this cover, corn is roasting on makeshift grills made from oil barrels split lengthwise. It puts Makiko in mind of a refugee tent, the kind she associates with undeveloped countries somewhere in Southeast Asia, where natives and stray dogs alike mill about waiting to be fed. The shock of this impression, coming as it does at this unguarded moment, awakens anew the shame of defeat.

"Ohhh-i!" Toshi yells out to one of his friends, and almost scampers off into the crowd before Makiko grabs him.

"Well," Makiko says, turning to her younger brother.

"That's the spirit!" Noboru says heartily, surveying the crowd. "Fall seven times, get up eight! Banzai! Banzai, for national rebuilding!" He proclaims this partly for Makiko's benefit and partly for that of a pretty young girl who is approaching them, no doubt a classmate of his. She has short hair with a permanent wave, like that of an American movie actress.

Standing in line with the young couple and a fidgety Toshi, Makiko wonders if the time will ever come when she can see a postwar substitute without the shadow of its former version.

But now, despite herself, she is distracted by the nearness of the corn, sizzling and crackling as the soy sauce and sugar drip into the flames. Her mouth waters. And when she finally takes her first bite, she is amazed to find it tastes exactly the way it did in her childhood, burnt outside and chewy inside. The surprise and relief of it bring tears to her eyes, and she chews vigorously to hide the sudden twisting of her features.

"This corn is so *good*, ne, Mama?" Toshi keeps saying, looking up from his rationed four centimeters of corncob. "This sure tastes *good*, ne?" The joy on his face, caught in the red glow of paper lanterns, is like a tableau.

"Yes, it's good," she says with pride, as if this is her own creation, her own legacy that she is handing down. "We ate food like this when your father was alive." She watches her son gnawing off the last of the kernels, sucking out the soy sauce from the cob. She hands him her own ration, from which she has taken but one bite.

"What a greedy piglet," Noboru teases, pretending to box his nephew's ears. Then he turns serious, remembering the girl beside him with the permanent wave. He is impressing her with his knowledge of astronomy. "Do you know which stars represent the separated lovers in that Tanabata legend?" he asks.

"I remember my father once pointing them out to me," the girl says. They are both gazing up at the sky, even though it is too early for stars. The girl gives a long sigh. "I've always loved that story," she says. "It's so sad and romantic, how once a year on Tanabata Night they're allowed to cross the gulf of the Milky Way, just for a few minutes, and be reunited again."

"The Western names for those stars," Noboru murmurs to her, "are Altair and Vega."

Later that night Makiko stands outside on her veranda, fanning herself with a paper *uchiwa*. Toshi is already asleep. The night garden is muggy; the mosquitoes are out in full force. She can hear their ominous whine from the hydrangea bush, in between the rasping of crickets, but they no longer target her as they did in her youth. She is thinner now, her skin harder from the sun, her blood watered down from all the rationing.

What a nice festival it turned out to be. More somber than in the old days, yet with remnants of its old charm. With the coming of the dark, the tent's harsh outlines had melted away and the red lanterns seemed to glow brighter. Shadowy forms gathered at the river's edge: adults bending over their children, helping them to hold out sparklers over the glassy water. The sparklers sputtered softly in the dark, shedding white flakes of light. Makiko had watched from a distance; Toshi was old enough, he had insisted, to do it by himself. She had remarked to Noboru how there is something in everyone that responds to fireworks: so fleeting, so lovely in the dark.

Right now the stars are out, although the surrounding rooftops obscure most of the night sky except for a full moon. She had noticed the moon earlier, at dusk, opaque and insubstantial. Now, through shifting moisture in the air, it glows bright and strong, awash with light, pulsing with light.

Surely tonight's festival owed its luster to all that lay beneath, to all those other evenings of her past that emit a lingering phosphorescence through tonight's surface. Which long-ago evenings exactly? . . . but they are slowly losing shape, dissolving within her consciousness.

Perhaps Toshi will remember this night. Perhaps it will rise up again, once he is grown, via some smell, some glint of light, bringing indefinable texture and emotion to a future summer evening. As will his memory of being carried by his father before an open window, or a time when he prayed before his father's picture.

Kami

AT BREAKFAST she plays Strauss waltzes, arias from *Carmen,* Italian classics such as "Santa Lucia" sung by robust, ardent men. And tangos: "La Cumparasita" in particular always brings her up off the floor cushion—where she sits alone at the low table eating miso soup, rice, salted salmon, and seaweed—to advance haughtily over the tatami matting, knees bent and one arm outstretched; then a snappy turn of the head (her aged body following more slowly) and a few more steps before sitting back down, heartbeat high. All it takes is music from when she was a bride—when she and her first husband, Shigeru, went ballroom dancing every Saturday night, in the years before the war took him away—for the vibrant, romantic young woman that she once was to flare up again, like dry kindling.

A widow of two years, Hanae has learned to utilize music with the same careful respect a medicine man gives his potions. She keeps two rice cracker tins filled with cassettes, all taped from the classical radio station and grouped by mood. Happy music works best in the morning, when a solitary day stretches before her like a long shadow. The elegant pace of traditional stringed koto is lovely for an afternoon tea break, when her chores are finished and she is feeling the satisfaction of a day used well. Every so often, however, especially if it happens to be raining outside, the meditative koto strains will cast a pall. In anticipation of this possibility she has scheduled her tea break for three o'clock, right before she leaves for the public bathhouse, the highlight of her day. And so Hanae listens with a serene heart: while washing tea utensils; while scurrying to pack her vinyl bag with washbasin, talcum powder, and soap; while setting the supper table for her return.

"Use music," she tells her youngest daughter, Kimiko, who comes visiting sporadically on weekends, "at crucial times in the day, to trick your mind into well-being." For Kimiko, Hanae recommends Edith Piaf. Frank Sinatra's love songs. Jazz from the big-band era, which has transcended her own generation. They are all available on the public radio station. "Clap your hands to this," she says as "Hanagasa Ondo," a Japanese peasant festival tune, plays on her portable radio–cassette player. "Just try it, hora. Clap, clap." Kimiko and her husband clap twice politely, then stop. Kimiko's two children, nine and eleven, pound their palms as fast and as loud as possible.

"But Grandma *said*!" they cry gleefully at their mother's glare.

"When something lifts your spirits, even for a few minutes," Hanae tells her harried daughter, raising her voice over the children's clapping, "like beautiful music, or a nice shade of lipstick, it raises the level of good hormones inside your body. And that starts a chain reaction. Better digestion, a better immune system. Therefore more protection against disease and senility."

Since her second husband, Daigo, died of esophageal cancer, Hanae has become something of an expert on health. Her knowledge comes from a popular NHK television program that airs weekdays at lunchtime. The show's host, Kenzo Uetani, presents multiple-choice questions to his celebrity guests, such as: Which fruit is most effective for preventing sinus infections—apple, orange, or banana? Yesterday afternoon the question was: Which part of the body, if massaged before bedtime, can lower blood pressure—foot, top of the thigh, or shoulder? Each celebrity took a guess, following it with a witty or coquettish rationale. The audience was polled. Finally the camera panned to a doctor in a conservative suit, looking slightly ill at ease among the vivacious media personalities. Each episode features a different doctor, perennially overqualified: Head of Hematology, Tokyo University Medical School; Head of Research, Kansai Cancer Institute. "The correct answer is the top of the thigh," the doctor announced, causing a twitter of amazement. He then proceeded to explain, in layman's terms, why this was so, showing simple diagrams of cells, blood vessels, and lymph nodes. He alluded to groundbreaking research unveiled at a medical symposium in Munich and published in America's *New England Journal of Medicine*.

Hanae jots it all down in a cheap student's notebook, consulting it later in order to fine-tune her diet, her exercise, her entertainments. *Moist environment crucial for warding off cold germs—boil water in kettle? fill vases with water? Iron more potent when taken with vitamin C—lemon juice with spinach? orange slice with everything? Keep dream journal: excellent mental benefits.*

Each new secret may yield days, even months, of additional life.

Last month, inspired by an episode about the effect of color on mood, Hanae redecorated her tiny bathroom: red gingham curtains, a pot of red plastic tulips in the corner, a red floor mat, red and white hand towels. For counterpoint, she hung a miniature teddy bear—brown—from the end of the light cord. The charged merriment of this room gives her a boost each time she enters, like wandering into Christmas in Europe. Assuming she uses the bathroom eight times a day for, say, an average of three minutes, in the course of a month that would add up to over ten hours of lifted spirits.

Hanae's sister-in-law Mitsu, eighty-one years old, is passing by Hanae's garden, shambling slowly and noisily through the alley gravel. Each Wednesday afternoon between two and three o'clock, she catches the bus to buy persimmon tea leaves from the Chinese herbalist. Hanae waters her arum lilies, which are managing to hold on despite the recent chill of autumn nights, and watches Mitsu's frail, bent body flashing in and out of view through the tall bamboo slats of the garden fence.

Two years ago, shortly after Hanae's second husband died, Mitsu had come to pay her respects. Even though she lived just two alleys away, she came shuffling through the gravel decked out in a formal kimono and matching zori slippers, ringing the bell at the visitors' gate instead of tapping on the kitchen door as usual. She knelt before Hanae in the guest room, her palsied fingertips resting on the tatami floor in prebowing position. "My little brother," she said, "did not deserve such a good wife. Daigo was gloomy and angry and *maaa,* nothing like your first husband, I'm sure. . . . Daigo used to be different, you know, before the war. But still, he gave you a hard life. Anyone would have understood if you'd shirked your duty near the end. But you are a fine woman . . . a fine woman, Hanae . . . please, accept my apologies and utmost respect." Then, going against standard etiquette—even though she was the elder of the two, as well as a relative on the husband's side—Mitsu had bowed down: not the routine forty-five-degree bow, but all the way down, until her head touched the floor.

Maaa, that someone like Mitsu should have the audacity to live so long. That whole family always got their own way. How graciously this woman humbled herself, so nobly apologizing for her little brother as if she hadn't been the one to coerce Hanae into that marriage to start with! Hanae breathed slowly and deeply as she bowed back, mindful not to activate the bad hormones. Flashes of latent anger did surface in her occasionally, but she was resigned to them, and kept them to herself. At this point in their lives, the two women had developed an easy acquaintance based on shared history and mutual advanced age.

Not like your first husband—if *that* wasn't the understatement of the Showa Period. Even nowadays, while cracking open a peanut (which is high in protein, vitamin E, and beneficial monounsaturated oil), Hanae thinks back fondly to the handsome young man who would superstitiously persist in hiding away peanuts from her while she was pregnant. "Peanuts and twin babies: both come two in a pod!" he warned when he was confronted. Shigeru lavished expensive substitutes upon her: dried white anchovies, fashionable imports such as buttered popcorn and bananas. Before their baby's unfortunate crib death, he even washed the diapers himself, hunching over the washtub in his summer underclothes. She never allowed Shigeru to hang up the wash in the yard, however; he would have lost face if the neighbors saw him doing women's work.

Years after her first husband died, Hanae would reminisce about him to Daigo. He listened grimly. "You think he'd be acting that way now, all playful and romantic and such, if he were still alive?" he had once roared at her, drunk on sake during a fight early on in their marriage. "What do you think happened to boys like that after years of jungle fever and prison camps? Stupid woman!" Hanae had turned up her nose and ignored him.

When Shigeru died in the war, Hanae had barely had time to grieve. Bombs dropped on their city, and she had managed to escape to a small city called O-Shige, whose inland location was safer. In her widowhood, Hanae was practically destitute. She had married a poor man, openly flaunting her family's wishes, and now pride kept her from crawling home to ask for help. Alone in this new city, Hanae scraped by on her widow's pension and on what meager savings her husband had left her, until Mitsu entered the scene.

Mitsu, a neighbor who for several months had been merely a polite acquaintance, accelerated their friendship one day with black market offerings of fabric, eggs, and soy beans. "My little brother has connections," she explained airily, and from that point on, she never missed a chance to praise Daigo, who had recently returned from the war. Hanae, naively gladdened by Mitsu's overtures of friendship, had accepted many such favors by the time homely Daigo took advantage of the situation to begin a courtship. Well, perhaps that was being unfair; no one had actually forced her to marry. But if she had only had more options! If only she hadn't indebted herself in that way to Mitsu, who had surely planned this in conjunction with her brother, then the outcome might have been different.

Delving too far into such memories, Hanae feels the bad hormones beginning to broil inside her body, the miasma of digestive juices rising up in her throat. The gerontologists on NHK are always warning her to think positive thoughts. Once you're old, they say, it takes very little to throw your mind and body out of kilter. With her knife, Hanae saws furiously at the arum lily stalk. She will put the flower in a vase on the family altar, then chant her evening sutras earlier than usual. By then, it should be time for the bathhouse to open.

For decades, Hanae had lived off the secret hope that her situation would change. She hadn't the slightest idea how, but who analyzes miracles? Some sudden spark of grace, emerging through the vagaries of chance. . . . But in the period after her second husband's funeral, Mitsu's condolences had brought home the truth: despite anything else fate might still hold in store, the basic outcome of Hanae's life was complete. Mitsu's formal dress and prostration had impressed this onto Hanae's mind like a huge red stamp on a shipping crate: Unfortunate Life. Dashed Hopes.

But in spite of everything, she does miss having her husband around the house. Ironies of life! Now Hanae is changing the water in the altar vase, throwing out last week's chrysanthemum, which has begun to shed, and replacing it with the arum lily from the garden. Actually Daigo wasn't such bad company in his last few years, illness and age having turned him rather docile. And he was the hub around which she had learned, out of necessity, to orbit. So what is the point now of cleaning house and cooking nice meals? But, a! a! That is a bad attitude. Things are getting better . . . for instance, at breakfast when she moves her body to the ballroom music. . . .

Hanae is a close observer of her elderly neighbors at the bathhouse. Drawing upon her steadily growing store of medical knowledge, she reconciles the state of their health to what she knows of their daily habits. Konishi-san, a mere sixty-seven, is a finicky eater. "I don't like the taste of eggs," she admits apologetically to the older women, lowering her head with proper obeisance. "Shabu-shabu beef sits like a lump in my esophagus. Raw vegetables are hard on my teeth." No wonder Konishi-san is always missing baths because of colds. There is an old saying from China: the key to good health is eating thirty different varieties of food a day.

Daigo was a difficult eater too, but in a different way; sometimes, when the depression overtook him, he would shut the shoji door to his office and refuse food for an entire day or two. And look what happened to him: cancer.

Ueno-san, a venerable eighty-five, lives in the weaving district on the other side of Daruma Boulevard. Her back is curved from all her years at the loom. But her naked body, seen from behind, is youthfully fleshy with a supple sheen. Ueno-san loves food; it is her favorite topic of discussion, and this afternoon she and Hanae are exchanging a catalog of everything they have eaten over the past week. Ueno-san has eaten braised eel, roast pork with noodles and green onions, lobster, and *hamachi* sushi from Niji-ya. High in vitamins and healthy monounsaturated fat—good, good (and high in price as well! Ueno-san's son, who left weaving for the merchandising business, must be doing extremely well lately).

"A certain amount of fat in the diet is essential," Hanae informs this small group of naked women. "One must never make the mistake, especially when elderly, of cutting healthy fats out of the diet."

"Soh, soh, I watched that episode too!" Ueno-san cuts in loudly, grinning with all her expensive dentures. Well! That is typical behavior coming from a simple, uneducated weaver's wife with the sensitivity of a potato and even less tact. It quite possibly accounts for her long healthy life as much as the food she eats.

There is actually much to be learned from these peasant types. Just the other day, Hanae heard of a new medical study suggesting that people with loud, unself-conscious voices have less danger of becoming senile than people with refined, timorous ones. That is something to consider, even though it goes against her entire upbringing. Hanae does not see herself as timorous, although she knows that in some ways she gives off that impression. For example, having lived in this city for over forty years, she still does not know her way to the downtown Civic Auditorium, or even to the famous Ryu Temple on the east side of the city. Hanae explains to the bathhouse women, and to her incredulous grandchildren, that she and her husband never went out much, and that when they did, she was always in the passenger seat thinking other thoughts.

But that is only part of the reason. Since her ignominious arrival here following her first husband's death and the bombing of her hometown, Hanae has always resented O-Shige. At first it was overt; she simply refused to familiarize herself with the city, in the same way a hostage would refuse to know his captor. Nowadays her antipathy is more unconscious; she vaguely pictures the unfamiliar areas as the desolate, war-ravaged neighborhoods of the forties. She still wakes from occasional nightmares in which she is wandering lost through silent, dilapidated streets where sorrowful ghostly forms float in and out of slatted wooden doorways. At any rate, through all these years Hanae has remained loyal to Kobe by the sea: to its carefree, cosmopolitan air before the war (aaa, those ballroom dance halls!), to the memory of strolling on a grassy cliff with Shigeru, gazing out at the sparks of light swarming over the water's green surface.

Hanae's immediate world, therefore, covers a two-kilometer area bounded at one end by Asahi Middle School, which her children once attended, and on the other, the Chinese herbalist at the end of Daruma Boulevard. Over the years, this neighborhood has not changed as rapidly as the rest of the city. Strolling home from the bathhouse, savoring the faint breeze on her freshly scrubbed skin, Hanae passes prewar homes still standing behind leaves of persimmon and bamboo, their wooden planks dark and weathered. Along the neighborhood's periphery, new office buildings, apartment complexes, and bus routes have sprung up. These recent developments have added to the *zatsu-on,* or background noise: a distant drone punctuated by a car horn or bicycle bell. It is a remote world out there, hazardous to aged pedestrians; Hanae knows its secrets only through television.

Living alone in her traditional Japanese home, open to the elements, Hanae has learned to value *zatsu-on.* The house provides no buffer against outside sounds such as the *k'sha k'sha* of alley gravel, by which she recognizes each neighbor from the force and rhythm of his footsteps, or, in early morning hours, the burble of pigeons. Hanae's sister, Tama, has a retirement home in Akashi—near Kobe—an expensive Western-style condominium on the third floor. Once, when Hanae went there to visit, she had shut the brand-new front door behind her and had the distinct impression of having sealed herself into an airtight box.

"If I lived in a place like that," Hanae often tells her friends at the public bathhouse, "I'd be senile by now, without a doubt." Sound connects her to life. This evening, she hears the melancholy *toohfu, tofu-tofu* of the tofu vendor's horn and thinks, as usual, Aaa, right now people are cooking supper. Later on tonight, when she lays out her futon, it will comfort her to hear old Mr. Kishi plucking away at his shamisen over in Murasaki Alley and always stumbling at the same point in the score.

A doctor on the NHK show once said that the quality of your life depends upon what links you maintain to life-enhancing forces.

Hanae's links are not merely auditory. Aside from the bathhouse, there are her daily strolls through the open-air market as well as her children's occasional visits. And there is the world of the past with all its happy memories, deliberately culled to keep down the bad hormones. There is the world of the dead, with which Hanae connects morning and evening through prayers at the family altar. There is the hope of longevity, which stimulates her each day when she turns to the NHK channel; her television is placed right next to the family altar (on a lower stand, of course, as is fitting). And there is her tiny garden, which for decades has been a source of pleasure and solace.

Daigo was the opposite, always shutting himself up like that in his dark office. Shortly before his diagnosis, back when Hanae was first discovering the health show, he had sighed and asked, "Why bother watching that? You know we're all going to die anyway." Now, knowing science as she does, she feels his cancer makes sense—he had refused to embrace those very links that might have kept him alive. In his last days, delirious from morphine, he had cried out, "There is no god! Anywhere!" and sobbed hoarsely for a minute or two until his drugged mind drifted off somewhere else. She cannot forget that. There is a lesson for her there.

More and more now, Hanae is on the lookout for mystical life-enhancing forces all around her. The precursors to the Shinto religion were shamans who spent the majority of their waking hours invoking, and revering, magical powers. They called those powers *kami,* that strange wisdom that presides over yeast rising or a fetus unfurling. The shamans believed everything was inhabited by *kami*—pine trees, rocks, a cooking fire, a handful of rice. She considers this now, slowly chewing her supper at the low table: innumerable vitamins and minerals and calories in each mouthful, mysteriously programmed to empower different parts of her body and mind. They can even join forces with other nutrients, as in the case of vitamin C and iron, for increased effectiveness. The NHK doctors, by validating such fantastic possibilities, have exposed her to a new realm of wonders. Aaa, they too are priests in their own right! Afterwards, waiting for sleep under her futon, Hanae ponders what she has learned from the show: that her body will repair itself as she lies here unconscious, digesting leftover food and knitting back together the minute muscle fibers torn during movement; that her nervous system, through cycles of dreams, will resolve emotion and memory into increasingly healthy patterns; each cell knowing, without her intervention, exactly what to do.

During the hot weather, Hanae had weeded and watered her garden right after breakfast, when the air was cool and her heart still buoyant from the ballroom music. Now that autumn is here, she waits till after lunch, when it is warmer. The smell of burning leaves wafts through the pale midday light of the alley. She has placed her portable radio–cassette player on the edge of the veranda, and koto music, turned to low volume, is trickling into the garden where she works.

Hanae's tall fluffy chrysanthemums are in full bloom, white and yellow and lavender, each flower as big as her hand. Most of the other flowers have gone the way of summer. The garden has a restrained, ascetic quality; gone is that wanton, wasteful lushness of summer growth. A new arum lily, a mere bud, has poked up amidst the browning, stiffening leaves, its waxy white petals still as fresh and firm as those of summer.

Freshly turned soil, according to a recent medical study, gives off beneficial minerals that, if regularly touched and inhaled, significantly strengthen one's immune system. This new bit of knowledge pleases Hanae immensely. She weeds and waters, solemnly inhaling the smoke-scented, beneficial minerals from the earth and fresh oxygen from her plants. She exhales carbon dioxide, which in turn nourishes the plants. Shafts of sunlight stream through the red maple leaves and press upon the back of her neck like warm fingers, infusing her body with vitamin D, which will strengthen her bones in concert with the calcium from today's lunch. Her stomach, meanwhile, is still digesting her meal—eleven different varieties of food—and vitamins are flowing through her digestive tract, being sorted and chemically altered and absorbed.

She recalls an educational television show in which a string of highly magnified cells bobbed slowly through the capillary of a leaf, as if in a trance.

This particular melody—reedy, punctuated by precise pluckings of the koto—is quite lovely. It evokes the spirit-summoning music of a shrine rite. Each cell of the music goes bobbing through the capillaries of her own mind, floating in a stream of good hormones. The melody seems to arise quite naturally from this somnolent afternoon, instead of from the cassette player on the veranda.

As a girl, Hanae used to take lessons in koto. But only now, especially in this last month or so, has she begun truly basking in its elegance and profundity. She admires the way each note has space in which to breathe, to reverberate within the mind, acting as syncopation to the mute mystery of things, as birdsong underscores the silence of a forest. Nothing can approach koto; certainly not Western music that, for all its dramatic surging and crashing (like that tiresome Beethoven, who gives her a headache), captures but life's surface, the turbulence of waves above a deep sea.

Hanae senses all this fleetingly, immersed beneath the surface of past sorrows thrashing above her with muffled sound. She senses with a certain awe how perfectly the music's pace matches that of the afternoon, and of digestion: the dappled leaf shadows moving over the earth like dark cells, the entirety of this garden harmonizing and fusing—plants, with carbon dioxide and sunlight; soil, with water from her plastic can; herself, with all the *kami* that have only now begun revealing themselves but have always existed, shifting and rotating in slow timeless patterns, like dancers of a classical age.

In the end, being alive is what matters.

Rationing

SABURO'S FATHER belonged to that generation which, having survived the war, rebuilt Japan from ashes, distilling defeat and loss into a single-minded focus with which they erected cities and industries and personal lives. Reflecting on this as an adult, Saburo felt it accounted at least partially for his father's stoicism. This was conjecture, of course. When Japan surrendered he had been only six, too young to remember what his father was like in peacetime.

Saburo's memories of the surrender included his uncle Kotai being brought home, delirious with hepatitic fever, from Micronesia. He lived for only a few weeks, unconscious the entire time and nursed round the clock by Saburo's parents. One of the visitors to their home was Uncle Kotai's sweetheart, a pretty girl of nineteen on whom Saburo had a crush. She wiped away her tears with a handkerchief patterned with cherry blossoms and announced brokenly that her life was now over. Saburo was impressed. "Big Sister really loves Uncle, ne!" he said later that day to his parents at dinner.

"The grief didn't hurt her appetite," his mother said curtly. She was referring to the rationed tea she had served at lunch, as well as to a certain fish cake that had been purchased, after two hours of waiting in line, for their family dinner.

In a dispassionate voice, Saburo's father explained that the amount of energy you have is limited, just like your food, and that when you love a sick person you have to make the choice of either using up that energy on tears or else saving it for constructive actions such as changing bedpans and spoon-feeding and giving sponge baths. "In the long run, which would help your uncle more?" he asked.

Saburo supposed the constructive actions would.

"That's right," his father said.

Saburo's father had not fought in the war. He was barred from service because of his glaucoma, which was discovered during his military recruiting exam. So he stayed home while the war claimed the lives of his best friend, then his cousin, and last of all his brother-in-law Kotai. Growing up, all Saburo understood of glaucoma was that it consisted of some sort of elevated pressure within the eye. "Your father has to keep calm," was his mother's constant refrain. "Don't you dare upset him, or his eye pressure will go up." It seemed to young Saburo that this condition was in some insidious way a result of the war, not unlike those radioactive poisons pulsing within survivors from Hiroshima.

At Uncle Kotai's funeral Saburo had overheard a woman say, "At least in his short life he was never thwarted." He understood later that Uncle, the babied youngest son of a wealthy family, had no profession save those of martial arts champion and dandy. He drank too often, laughed too loudly, used too much hair pomade. Saburo had very few memories of him or of their former wealth, which had been lost in the Tenkan bombing, forcing Saburo's family to move into the merchant district. He did recall that once when he had gotten a nosebleed as a little boy, Uncle Kotai stopped it instantly by giving a hard chop with the side of his hand to a specific vertebra on his nape. "Aaa, be careful!" Saburo's mother had wailed, watching with both hands pressed to her mouth. Uncle Kotai used another trick when Saburo tried to tag along on one of his outings. "Let me come, I want to go too!" he had demanded, squatting at his uncle's feet and clutching fistfuls of his long *yukata*. With a rumble of amusement, Uncle Kotai reached down to press some secret nerve between thumb and forefinger, and Saburo's fists miraculously unclenched.

Seen across the gulf of the war that separated them, this lost uncle held for young Saburo all the magic of a lost era, a magic emanating from the smallest of details: a photograph of Uncle and his well-dressed friends sitting around a heavily laden banquet table, heads thrown back in laughter, or his mother's nostalgic recounting of Uncle's outrageous pranks. The aura of careless abundance often wafted up around him, faint and nebulous. Yet running through this wonder was a hard thread of moral disapproval. Uncle had it coming. Saburo had overheard his mother telling a neighbor that Uncle Kotai had been born in the year of the rooster. Roosters, as Saburo knew, finished their crowing early in the day.

~§~

When Saburo joined the track and field team in his first year at Bukkyo High School, the sport was enjoying a popularity it had not known before the war. At the time, few schools could afford baseball bats or gymnastic equipment. And there was something in the simplicity of the sport—the straight path to the goal, the dramatic finish line—that stirred the community to yells and often tears. On Sundays entire families came outdoors to cheer, thermoses of cold wheat tea slung across their chests. They sat on woven mats and munched on rice balls, roasted potatoes, hard-boiled eggs, and pickled shoots of *fuki* gathered up in the hills.

"So what distance are you running?" Saburo's father asked at the dinner table.

"Eight hundred meters," Saburo said. He would have preferred a long-distance event, which commanded the most respect. But he had watched those runners stagger toward the finish line, eyes rolling back in their heads, some even vomiting in the grass afterwards—and he had been afraid. Sprints came next in popularity, but Saburo was not particularly fast. Two laps around the track seemed the most appropriate distance.

"Eight hundred meters? Nothing else?"

"I just want to focus on one," Saburo said, "and perfect it."

His father nodded in approval.

Saburo's father was old, much older than his mother. His gray hair, ascetic cheekbones, and scholarly decorum (he was professor of astronomy at Nangyo University) commanded both respect and distance. When sitting down beside his father at the low dining table, Saburo encountered moments of readjustment similar to entering a temple from a busy street. Dinner-table conversations, more often than not, were monologues on the moons of Jupiter, the Andromeda nebulae, or various theories on cosmogony. Chewing his food slowly—a habit from rationing days, when the rule had been one hundred times— Saburo let the academic words flow through him like water through a net. What he heard was his father's voice: a voice like the universe, regulated and unknowable, with the endurance of silent planets rotating in their endless, solitary orbits.

Something about the running must have struck a chord with his father, although as far as Saburo knew, he had not been a track man in his youth. At any rate, the following evening at dinner his father made an announcement. "On the days you don't have practice," he told Saburo, "I'll be taking you out to Kaigane Station to clock your runs."

Saburo's mother looked up from scooping rice into a bowl. "Maa, Father, what an excellent idea!" she said. She then turned to her son, surprise and pleasure still in her face. "Saburo, thank your father," she said. Saburo was not altogether happy with the arrangement; his devotion to running was not that strong. Nonetheless, he was suffused with a quiet manly pride that he tried to mask with an expression of nonchalance. "So nice, ne—a father and son, doing things together!" sang Saburo's mother, expecting no reply and getting none besides a good-willed "That's right" from her husband. Dinner that night felt very much like a rite of passage, and Saburo's mother served up the mackerel with a gravity reserved for celebratory red snappers.

Saburo's father never attended Saburo's track competitions; he left that to his wife. But he always inquired after the results at dinner, showing more interest in his son's times than in his rankings—a good thing, since Saburo never placed especially high. The boy never thought to question his father's absences or to complain. His father was simply different. He was old. He was an academic, whereas Saburo's friends' fathers were grocers and merchants. If he got excited, his eye pressure would go up.

But from that evening on, each time Saburo came home on nonpractice days, his father was waiting, still dressed in his Western-style lecture clothes: white short-sleeved shirt and gray trousers, creased and starched. They sat gingerly side by side in the streetcar as it bumped and clattered through the bustling fish vendors' district, the smells and raucous vendor calls floating in through the windows. It was awkward and silent in the streetcar, just the two of them. Saburo's mother, with her cheerful chatter, so often served as their buffer. Saburo stole a glance at his father, who was carefully holding both their tickets ready in one hand, even though there were still a dozen stops left to go. He wished his father were like his friends' fathers: sun-browned, guffawing men who ruffled children's hair with affectionate ease.

The streetcar rattled on until there was no more open-air market, only an asphalt road slicing through kilometer after kilometer of rice paddies. Kaigane train station was the final stop on the route. As a result of postwar cutbacks the train came through only once a day now, so in the evenings the station was deserted.

Only here, with silence stretching over the open fields like a vast extension of his father's presence, did Saburo feel complete harmony between them.

Saburo took his place at the makeshift starting line exactly 800 meters south of the platform (they had measured it out on the first day, using a 100-meter ball of string). His father waited back at the platform, a slight, gaunt figure next to the metal station billboard. As he peered at his wristwatch, clutched in both hands, Saburo raced toward him on the asphalt. A sea of rice plants, dyed red from the sunset, undulated on either side. On those spring evenings, the sharp green smell of growing things stung Saburo's nostrils as he sucked it in, and pierced his lungs like frosty air. His elongated shadow floated beside him with effortless strides, like a long, fluid ghost. If he suddenly stopped running, his shadow might have kept on going.

"Two-forty-nine," his father said. Saburo panted, leaning over with hands on knees, waiting to regain his wind so he could run it again. Somewhere in the paddies, frogs were croaking.

"Are you pacing yourself?" his father asked. "Remember, it doesn't matter who's in front of you. Beating your own time's all that matters. You can do that with practice. So don't be affected by those other runners. You just keep on improving, slow and steady." Everything his father did was slow and steady. Saburo pictured how he might run: rationing each breath, timing each footfall, looking neither left nor right at anything else around him.

Saburo quit the team after one year, in order to devote his second and third years to tutoring sessions for college entrance examinations. His father said gravely that it sounded like a fine idea. Despite his relief—he had never really liked the running or its accompanying pressures—Saburo felt guilty over ending their sessions, which he sensed his father had enjoyed and wished to continue. He had the sad premonition they would never again have a similar experience. As it turned out, the sessions could not have continued anyway; within a year, Kaigane Station's activity increased, along with the upswing in Japan's economy, and the surrounding fields gave way to construction sites for future buildings.

Over the next few years prosperity continued, bringing with it an increase in motorbikes and automobiles—menaces in the cluttered, swarming alleyways of the merchant district. Saburo's mother was a casualty of one such motorbike as it made a sharp turn around the corner near the seaweed grocer's. She died several hours later on the hospital operating table.

Saburo was nineteen at the time, home from the university for New Year's vacation. He and his father took a taxi to Shinjin Municipal Hospital as soon as they heard of the accident. Mutely they waited on a bench in the hallway, faces blanched from the blue fluorescent light. The doctor finally arrived, told them "nothing could be done to save her," lingered a respectable interval, then hurried away to his duties.

Saburo turned to his father. He was hunched forward with his elbows on his knees, gazing down into his dangling hands, which showed the beginnings of liver spots. He seemed to have forgotten his son's presence. "Father—" Saburo said. There was no response. The awkward streetcar rides flashed into his mind, and in that moment of panic he understood himself to be on the verge of something he had feared, subconsciously, all his life. Lifting his hand, Saburo rested it on the middle of his father's back. Despite the gravity of the situation, his gesture felt ill-timed and melodramatic. There was no response through the scratchy wool of his father's sweater. Saburo lowered his hand to his side.

When they got home from the hospital, Saburo's father stopped before the calendar hanging above the kitchen counter, above a bowl of water in which kelp strips were still soaking for that night's dinner. With a black ballpoint pen, his father drew a big firm X over the box for the twenty-eighth day. "December twenty-eighth," he said, retracing the X over and over, with growing force. "This was a bad, *bad* day." Each time Saburo passed the calendar, that black X jumped out at him from an otherwise empty month, the tips of four neat triangles curling outward from where the ballpoint pen had sliced through the paper.

In the ensuing weeks, Saburo had a recurring dream about high school track. In this dream two runners were ahead of him but not by much, and it was only the first lap; he was positioned right where he wanted to be. But wait. The crowd was cheering too much for just the first lap. Then he knew, as one does in dreams, that he had made a mistake. This was not the 800. This was the 400.

Eventually, however, he was rescued by the memory of one long-ago Mother's Day, when he had presented his mother with a necklace he had woven from sweet peas and clover. She had exclaimed over it, then added, "But the best present you can give me is good grades so that someday you'll do well at the university and make your country proud." What a letdown that had been at the time. But now her words glowed hot in his brain, and for the first time Saburo understood how loss could resolve itself through complex transfers of emotion. Back at

school, subdued but focused, he immersed himself in his engineering studies.

His father, meanwhile, altered his domestic routine: Each
night at six, he strolled to the *oden* cookery, where he chewed
his dinner, calm and controlled as always; on Friday evenings
he dropped off his clothes at the launderer's. The rhythm of
this new schedule suggested years of familiarity, as if no prior
way of life had existed. Saburo remembered, with a pang, the
seamless way his father had replaced their running sessions
with paperwork. Over the next few months, when Saburo came
home on his increasingly brief visits, he noted the gradual dis-
appearance of his mother's effects—with the exception of one
framed photograph beside the family altar—leaving the house
monkish and austere, a mirror of his father.

Saburo pondered the fact of his parents' arranged marriage.
Did that lessen the heartbreak? Once, his father, while turning
down the volume of a *Madame Butterfly* aria swelling forth from
the radio (he was not a fan of Italian opera, which was "full of
ego"), had muttered, "True love, true love . . . who even knows
what that means?" Saburo could not tell if a response was
expected.

Yet years after his wife might have faded from memory,
Saburo's father mentioned her, if only in passing, each time his
son came visiting: "Now your mother, on a day like this she
would have loved sitting out here in the garden." Saburo
thought how much easier it would have been if their emo-
tions—his and his father's—had been realized, apportioned,
and spent, in their entirety, over his mother's lifetime.

At thirty, Saburo was doing well for himself. He held a respected position at a civil engineering firm. After years of saving he had purchased a Western-style condominium in the up-and-coming Kiji district, built over those fields where he had once run. A handsome man, with something of his Uncle Kotai lurking about the lips, Saburo attracted women with an ease he did not fully understand. It required little effort: some lighthearted banter, which came easily in adulthood, and on occasion a calculatedly mischievous grin. Given his unremarkable past, this was gratifying to his self-esteem. "Takes after Kotai-san," said one elderly woman from his old neighborhood. But unlike his uncle, Saburo did nothing in excess, not even banter. Perhaps it was this restraint that attracted the women. At any rate, Saburo was in no rush to marry; there was plenty of time. Life was pleasant and under control. On weekends he swam laps with sure, unhurried strokes.

Around this time, his father's glaucoma began giving him trouble. Over the decades its pressure had increased steadily despite medication, and several years ago a severe migraine required his right eye to be replaced with a glass one whose chestnut hue was a close, but not exact, match with the more faded brown of his left eye. Now his peripheral vision in the remaining eye had disappeared to the point where his father could see only what was directly before him, as if looking at the world through a narrow pipe. During one of his sporadic visits, Saburo saw how his father patted the air around him like a blind man. He proposed—in the same quiet way his father had once announced the running sessions—that he visit his father every Sunday, at which time he would take care of all grocery shopping and outside errands. Afterwards he would escort his father on a walk through the neighborhood streets, which were too dangerous now for a frail, half-blind man in his seventies. His father's ready acquiescence, in contrast to his usual self-sufficiency, indicated how grave the situation must have been.

And so a new routine began. They strolled in the afternoons, through narrow alleyways where morning glory vines, their blooms shrunk to purple matchsticks in the afternoon sun, cascaded over old-fashioned bamboo lattices. It became second nature for Saburo to walk two steps ahead on flat surfaces; otherwise his father, with his tunnel vision, would lose track of him entirely. Occasionally in the alley they met a housewife who stopped her sweeping to bow watchfully as the pair passed: the younger man taking slow, tiny steps, the distinguished-looking old gentleman shuffling close behind him.

Now that Saburo was an adult, their conversations were no longer awkward. Any conversational opening inevitably led to a lecture on astronomy, thus little was required on Saburo's part. He felt relaxed, self-assured in the knowledge of all he was doing for his father. At appropriate pauses, he made a comment over his shoulder ("That kind of magnitude is hard to grasp") or asked a question ("And how was that discovery received by the scientific community?"). His father, he realized, had a passionate side. At rare intervals, when he was caught up in some obscure detail, the old man's voice rose with fervor and he came to a full stop in order to make his point. Saburo pictured his father as a student in some university teahouse, robed in good-quality silks and ardently discussing science, ideals, the future of the world. It was a brief, fragrant whiff of that prewar world of which Saburo had never been a part.

Sometimes he discussed his own work—the new railroad

they were currently building through the Hiei pass—or else he inquired after his father's routine, which seemed to consist largely of scientific reading interspersed with eye exercises, radio news programs, and long sitting sessions in the garden. But as time passed, Saburo dwelled less and less on such mundane topics. He began looking forward to his father's monologues, which at first he had tolerated out of filial duty. They filled him now with a sense of wonder, of vast sweeps of time and space and human endeavors and intellectual possibilities. They reminded him somehow of those open fields of his childhood. On his way home after these visits, riding the bus through the open-air market—which at that hour was cluttered and bustling in the warm red glow of paper lanterns—Saburo was keenly, inarticulately, aware of the sky beyond, purpling and darkening.

An exception to this companionable routine came several days after a quarterly eye checkup. His father's range of vision had dropped, not by one-half to one point as expected, but by two points and a quarter. "If I go blind now, at my age," his father remarked gravely as they shuffled their way along the alley, "I plan to end my life."

Saburo froze. With anyone else he would have said all the right things: "Don't be silly! There's always something to live for! I love you and I'm here for you!" He was good at such gestures, especially with women. But someone like his father must not be insulted by such clichés. This was not a cry for pity but a non-negotiable decision related out of courtesy. Saburo knew his father must have pondered this alone for months, weighing the pros and cons in his academic fashion.

After a few minutes Saburo asked, "How would you do it?"

"With a gun. Very simple, just hold it to your ear and pull the trigger."

"Not something easier," he asked tentatively, "like gas or sleeping pills?"

"Those don't work right away. Someone finds you halfway through, then they've got you in the hospital, making a big fuss. You come out of it half paralyzed, brain-damaged."

Saburo said nothing. They walked silently. The alley was deserted, and the early autumn sunlight slanted down, reddish, at a low angle. They approached the Sunemuras' olive tree, whose branches leaned out over the old-fashioned adobe wall of their garden and shaded the alley. Waiting for his father to reach his side, Saburo cupped his hand behind his father's sweatered elbow as they passed beneath the olive branches, steering him around the slippery black pulp of overripe olives that had dropped onto the cement. He did this every time they passed the olive tree, although his father's refusal to lean on him, to physically acknowledge the assistance in any way, made Saburo remove his hand the moment they were in the clear.

"That's life, Saburo." His father's voice was as grave and modulated as ever. "And your time will free up. There's nothing wrong with that. You need more than a busy job and a sick parent."

They walked. From somewhere in the distance came a faint smell of burning leaves.

Then his father launched easily, noncommittally, into a deploration of this week's radio series on Mars. "Life . . . on . . . Mars!" he said dryly, mimicking the radio host's dramatic tone. "Hehh, they can't even present simple facts without dramatizing them all out of proportion."

Only now did Saburo notice that the underarms of his own imported linen shirt were damp with sweat. He thought he had outgrown this terror from the day of his mother's death, when he had reached over to touch his father's back. His mother would have known what to do. Mother. . . . Once when Saburo was in the first grade, she had gripped his face between her hands and, driven by some intense, private emotion, kissed the top of his shaved head with furious pecks.

After the visit with his father, on the bus ride home, Saburo reviewed the situation realistically. Outsiders would not understand their exchange. They would not see that his father, far from begging for sympathy, would have considered it out of place. The truth was that there was an understanding; they had no need for embarrassing displays. Saburo thought of the railroad they were drafting at work, its parallel rails never touching, yet exquisitely synchronized, committed in their separateness as they curved through hill and valley. That, he was comfortable with. That, he could do.

His father's cancer, a year later, came as a complete surprise. The possibility of another disease had never occurred to Saburo; there was simply no room for it. It began when his father telephoned him early one morning, his voice fainter than usual yet admirably steady, to say he had terrible stomach cramps and could Saburo escort him to the emergency room? Never before had his father called him at home. "No need to bother you," he always said. "It can wait till Sunday."

Doctors sedated his father for the rest of the day; they took X rays and informed Saburo that a large tumor was obstructing his colon. An emergency colostomy was performed. "Terrible!" said one doctor around Saburo's age, shaking his bristly head and peeling off his rubber gloves. "The cancer's spread all over the place. The white cell count is incredible! Why wasn't it caught before?"

"My father doesn't like doctors," Saburo said.

The young doctor made a knowing grimace. "That generation, well," he said.

Waiting for his father to regain consciousness after the operation, Saburo stood before the window in the little hospital room, alternately peering back over his shoulder at his father's bed and gazing out at the city below. The landscape had changed since he had been here last. In his youth, dusk would have melted those distant hills to smooth lines like folded wings. Tonight, against a fading sky of pink and gray, the sharp black silhouette of the hills bristled with crooked telephone poles. The hills themselves were spattered with mismatched lights. *The rate of progress,* he recalled someone, somewhere, saying.

"What happened?" his father murmured within the first few minutes of coming to. Saburo had to bend over to hear him. He was attached to an oxygen tube, an IV, and an ancient machine with rather grimy indicator knobs. The machine filled the room with a soft, continuous roar.

"Everything's taken care of, Father," Saburo said. He explained about the colostomy.

"I don't have to use this bag for the rest of my life, do I?"

The truth was his father had only a few months left to live. That news could wait till tomorrow. "I'm afraid you will, Father," Saburo said.

"Oh . . ." A sigh like a deflating balloon, then silence.

The following day Saburo had no chance to break the news; specialists were performing tests most of the day. For lunch, Saburo ate a plate of curry in the hospital cafeteria. Through the glass wall, he watched nurses striding by in the hall, clipboards pressed against their chests. The sight of them—the very smell of this place—stirred up memories of his mother's death; he was conscious now, as he had been then, of his utter uselessness. From now on, it was the nurses and doctors who would do everything, to whom his father would turn for help. *Which would help your uncle more?* he remembered his father saying.

"One of them told me the results," his father reported that evening. "Quiet fellow, very nice." Sipping miso soup from a styrofoam cup, his father recounted the details of the cancer that had already metastasized to his stomach, lymph nodes, and lungs. "The doctor recommends," his father said, "a small place in Fuji-no with round-the-clock medical staff . . ." He was tiring now, taking short, shallow breaths. " . . . and dietitians. That'll work out best for everybody. It won't be for long."

If only he could have broken the news to his father. If only he could have caught the spontaneous reaction, however minute! He saw ahead to how his father would die, as courteous and restrained in his final hours as he had been in his life. Saburo had expected more: a brushfire that would drive some vague, crouching thing out of hiding. He had dreaded an onset of naked emotion, had pushed it off to the future when he would be better prepared, but never, he realized now, had he considered the possibility of it not happening.

That night, Saburo dreamed he came across his mother in

the alley, playing jump rope in her apron with some neighborhood girls. Strands had come loose from her bun, and she was flushed, laughing. She noticed him and said brightly, "Ara, ara! Is it time already?"

"Mama! There you are!" Saburo cried out. Such relief surged through him that it lifted him out of sleep. As he lay awake in the dark, it took him several moments to comprehend that his mother had been gone for years.

Saburo did what he could. He ate well, three meals a day. He cut back drastically on his work hours. He curtailed his social life, although on occasion he lightened his routine by inviting a girl to accompany him to the movie theater. He deliberately chose comedy: *Teppan-gumi* or foreign films featuring Charlie Chaplin.

Nonetheless, the situation took its toll. The old track-and-field nightmare returned. Unable to fall back asleep, Saburo tossed and turned, seeing before him his father's glass eye crusted over with yellow mucus, as it had once looked when a nurse forgot to wash it out with eyedrops. Or he saw him wearily close his eyes and whisper, "Thank you," after a nurse changed his colostomy bag.

By now his father was installed in the recommended Fuji-no hospital for terminally ill patients. He had little strength—he had never quite recovered from the operation—and he fought to sit up, even to shift position on the bed. Still, he courteously attempted conversation. "How are you holding up, Saburo?" he asked each evening, as if his son were the ailing one. To save his father's energy, Saburo did most of the talking. Then, running out of topics, he took to reading to his father from *History of the Cosmos,* a book he had found on his father's desk at home. There was something soothing about reading aloud; all meaning dropped away, and he was borne along on a cadence reminiscent of boyhood, when his father's voice had washed over him at the dinner table.

One evening the reading lulled his father to sleep. Saburo gazed at the drawn, wasted face. The hospital was silent—it might have been midnight instead of seven o'clock. If Saburo stared long enough in the eerie fluorescence of overhead lights, the pallid face with its sunken eye sockets became that of a corpse.

Above the blanket, his father's hand twitched in sleep. It was the surreal quality of this moment—a tenuous balance of his father's unconsciousness, the temporary absence of night nurses, the lingering effects of reading about an impersonal cosmos— that made Saburo reach out with one finger, and touch his father's hand. Its folds were cold and surprisingly loose, like sea cucumbers he had once poked as a boy in the open-air market. The forearm was warmer, but so much smaller, so much more frail between Saburo's fingertips, than eyesight had prepared him for. Saburo went on to trace the bony blade of a gowned shoulder. This felt like a violation and it made him nervous: was his father really asleep? Maybe he was conscious behind those closed lids. Maybe the touching bothered him but he was too polite, or too weak, to react. But Saburo couldn't stop. He couldn't help himself.

The physical contact dissolved some hard center of logic within him. And Saburo wondered, with sudden urgency, whether his father was really as self-sufficient as he had always assumed him to be. Might his father have hoped for a different reaction the day he talked of suicide? Might he have longed for closeness but not known how to go about it? Unlikely, but still . . . dangerous thoughts.

Saburo had made the best decisions he could, as his father had, surely, with all his careful ways. But warped by circumstance and changing worlds, compounded by time and habit, the results had come up short. It was inevitable. The longer one's life, the more room it left for errors of calculation.

If things had been different he might have told his father, as other sons surely did, "I admire you more than anyone I've ever known. For your intellect, for your great dignity." If such words were possible, he would have felt only the clean, sharp arrows of pain; there would have been a rightness to it all, a bittersweet perfection of a setting sun. What Saburo felt now bordered on nausea, which had always terrified him. He had thrown up only two or three times as a child, but he still remembered that instant of panic when it all came rising up, unstoppable—too strong a flood for one narrow windpipe.

His father's eyes opened. "Saburo?" he whispered.

"I'm here, Father," Saburo said. He stilled his hand, keeping it over his father's icy hand. It occurred to him that his father would not be able to feel this. Poor circulation in the extremities, the nurse had told him, causes numbness.

"Aaa, it's you . . . ," his father said.

"Father," Saburo began. He stopped. His Adam's apple was constricting, shot through with the ache, long-forgotten yet familiar, of impending tears. He waited until it subsided.

"Father," he said in a rush. "I'm not good at saying fancy things." His throat closed up again, and he sat helpless.

His father's good eye had turned toward his son's voice, the pupil shrunken to pinpoint from glaucoma medication. Saburo felt a great mute pain open out in his chest. It reminded him of track days: anguish escalating unbearably in oxygen-deprived lungs, the blind rush down the homestretch on legs that were too slow.

The Laws of Evening

ONLY AFTER the last tour bus had rumbled out of the parking area into Shimbonmachi Boulevard did the temple grounds revert to what they had been when Japan was a poor country. The nine temple buildings, which in daytime held themselves aloof and historical behind government-issued iron railings, seemed now in the empty hush of twilight to deflate, to sink back to earth among the darkening pines, taking second place to the emerging sounds of nightfall: outbursts of crows in the gnarled branches; gurglings of pigeons waddling over deserted flagstone paths, searching the cracks for something overlooked. In this dusk Sono strolled alone, occasionally passing a robed monk raking gravel beside the path.

She had lived in this neighborhood for almost eighty years. When she was small—no, even as recently as when her daughters were alive—children had played here freely, their nimble brown legs chasing each other up and down the long wooden verandas of the temple buildings or climbing the pine trees in search of crows' eggs. Decades ago, one of the Uemura boys had fallen out of a tree, pecked in the face by a frenzied mother crow appearing out of nowhere.

Her twin girls, Haruko and Natsuko, had played near the *jizo*—stone statues of child Buddhas. Ten of them stood smiling in a small dirt clearing, their faces half rained away; most dated back to the Edo Period in the seventeenth century. An amateur historical society had collected these relics in the 1930s from remote farming villages in the outlying Hiezan hills, only to abandon them here in the temple grounds in the crisis of the Second World War. To this day the *jizo* stood—or so Sono assumed—hidden from sight behind a thatched groundskeeping shed, awaiting administrative action.

Once she had caught Haruko and Natsuko playing there, no taller than the statues: offering them water and flowers, just as Sono did each day before the family altar at home; laying out tiny mud balls skewered on pine needles. Even their dolls sat propped up against the *jizo,* smiling above bright red bibs torn from rice paper: imitations of the religious cotton bibs that the statues wore.

"S'a s'a, come away from there!" Sono had said sharply. "Right now! Don't get too close!" Leading away the reluctant children, one with each hand, she tried to explain. "In the old days," she said, "people from the hills would make a *jizo-san* for babies whose ashes couldn't be buried in a family plot like everybody else. It's all too sad to explain, but I'm telling you: there's bad karma in those statues, ne? It's best to just keep away completely. Do you understand? Bad spirits are hanging around there." And, as the little girls' eyes flew up to hers in protest, "Ara! You don't believe me? I'm telling you the truth. Those spirits are sad and lonely and full of ill will, because nobody chanted sutras for them, and now they can't leave the earth to go on to the next world. You keep playing there, and their bad luck's going to follow *you* . . ." Sono bent down to whisper the ominous "you" into Haruko's ear—for she was the leader of the two—and the child jerked back slightly in alarm. "Is that what you want?" She had pictured them coming home with unsavory spirits trailing behind them, like mangy stray dogs.

Sono was not a superstitious woman by nature; deep down, she knew they were just old wives' tales. But during wartime, it seemed important to take precautions. So much was at stake, balanced on a scale that could tip at the slightest touch: the twin girls, born frail to begin with and now verging on malnutrition since the food rationing; Sono's husband, still fighting with the ground troops in Burma; those prized Chinese chrysanthemums he had left behind in her care always wilting at the slightest shift in temperature; her entire teetering world of present and future.

Nonetheless, when her girls contracted food poisoning from sharing a spoiled red bean bun; when the food poisoning eventually subsided, only to trigger some mysterious new fever that surpassed 43 degrees despite the ice water baths; when the delirious children died in her arms within a week of each other, four months after their sixth birthday, Sono understood that *jizo* were not to blame. There were many new diseases in Japan now. Wounded soldiers were coming home after being exposed to bacteria from strange, unsanitary lands: Burma, mainland China, the Philippine Islands. In addition this was June, rainy season—when such bacteria would be most rampant, when the air lay on your skin like damp laundry all month long and mildew bloomed overnight, black and green and ashy pink: between ceramic tiles, on the edges of dish towels wrung out to dry, inside day-old clumps of dearly gotten rice.

By the time they had transferred her husband's name from the list of Missing in Action to Killed in Action, the *jizo* were no longer an issue.

Occasionally when Sono walked with her cane through the temple yard in the failing light, past the temples and that little shed behind which the *jizo* no doubt still stood in their faded red bibs, she thought of Haruko and Natsuko. After this many years, it was like peering down through a cloudy pond at something whose outline had melted away. Once in a long while, though, it would stir. A slow bubble would float up to the surface and burst, releasing an image so achingly vivid that, even now, her heartbeat quickened with astonished recognition. . . .

Two small, identical girls with square bobs, glancing up in guilty surprise as they squatted before their mud balls: a streak of dirt along Natsuko's chin, their round cheeks stained pink from the autumn wind.

Sono was not, in her own view, a religious woman. However, each morning and evening she placed rice and water before the family altar, burning half a stick of incense each time and chanting sutras in a practiced, efficient voice. The flowers at the altar she changed once a week. Whatever her own doubts might be of the afterlife, it was not her place to impose them upon her loved ones and deprive them of sutras that might make all the difference to them, wherever they were. The altar tablets—miniature bronze headstones with four tiny clawed feet, consecrated each September by a monk—had taken on increasing significance over the years, as the essence of her husband and children faded from the surrounding alleys and even from these very rooms.

After the sutras, Sono often addressed the tablets as if they were people—but only those of her husband and daughters, lined up in front near the rice and water, not those of her in-laws and her husband's other relatives, crammed together to the back. "After breakfast today," she might say, "I'm taking the bus over to the Takashimaya department store. You watch over me, ne? Stop me if I start any impulse spending."

"You should be spending more time around people," a widowed neighbor told her at the public bathhouse, scrubbing her back for her while she sat on a plastic stool. "What about the senior citizens' center, O-Sono-san? It's right off Shimbonmachi, near the open-air market. It's free."

"Saa, I don't know," Sono said. On the other side of the dividing wall rose a sudden burst of men's laughter. She glanced up as always, knowing there was nothing to see but steam pouring over the tiled wall from the other side, as echoes of the men's laughter hung bobbing from the high domed ceiling.

"But, O-Sono-san! I highly recommend it. *We've* all been going to the moss gardens at Ten-jin-san, playing croquet, learning sumi-e painting . . . this spring we even went up to the Hiezan hills to see the gorgeous cherry blossoms. We soaked in the mineral baths there! The government *pays* for it. It's free. You should make an effort, O-Sono-san, especially now that Akimi's gone and you're all by yourself."

Akimi was Sono's niece who, for over forty years, had been living in Sono's house. She had moved in a few years after the death of Sono's husband. Akimi was widowed also, a gentle woman with three small boys; she and Sono had been companions all these years, raising the boys together and living frugally off their husbands' pensions. But recently Akimi's elder son had taken a wife, and his mother had gone to live with them, as was fitting, somewhere in Aomori Prefecture.

"The truth is," Sono said, yawning from the heat of the steam, "I feel like it's too late in life for me to be taking an interest in all these kinds of things."

"Ara, O-Sono-san . . . ," her friend said disapprovingly. Sono felt the pressure on her back change from solicitous stroking to a brisk scrub, as if to scour her passivity away. "What an unhealthy attitude, with all due respect. Maa, the doctors on that NHK health show are always saying! They're saying: talk to young people, join the social groups. Get a little pet! Keep yourself involved, that's what they're saying. Right up till the last minute, ne? When we get old we should never, never be allowing ourselves the chance to brood."

Maybe so, Sono thought, and as she was brooding about it July rolled along, and with it the fiftieth anniversary of her husband's death. At two o'clock on Tuesday the twenty-first, she attended an official thirty-minute sutra chant at a temple on the other side of town. The twins' fiftieth had been taken care of a month earlier. Now no more anniversaries were required. Sono rode home on the bus that afternoon feeling curiously devoid of emotion, the gong's aftermath still wavering in her ears. She had done them all: first, third, seventh, thirteenth, thirty-third, fiftieth; each anniversary breaking yet another link binding the spirits to this earth, until they rose up and away like helium balloons. She had done her duty. Now they were far away in a safe place, out of danger beyond any possible doubt.

Sono was taking a shortcut home through an empty section of the temple grounds when exhaustion suddenly struck. She dropped her parasol and gripped her cane with both hands—a sturdy bamboo, fortunately, with a broad rubberized base. She felt gravity dragging at her knees, threatening to bring her crumpling down onto the flagstones. The curved handle of the cane shook in her hands. Sono focused hard on a line of small black ants wending their way across the flagstones, carrying in their jaws what appeared to be grains of sand, and eventually the danger passed.

She was shaken, and needed to sit down. But there were no benches. Tourists were encouraged to linger only within the old-fashioned teahouse outside the main gate, which sold cold wheat tea and miso dumplings at outlandish prices. Too far away. The groundskeeping shed was just a few meters off the path—hadn't there once been a bench near the *jizo,* under a tree? Sono picked up her parasol and shuffled through the gravel to the thatched shed, going around it, then following the short dirt trail, just as she had done decades ago but much more slowly now, forging past long summer grasses that leaned over and caught at her stockings with their jagged edges.

She stayed on the bench longer than was necessary, absently pressing her handkerchief to the perspiration on her face and neck. The sun still shone strong. From the surrounding pines, cicadas were shrilling *meeeee;* the sound shimmered endlessly in the still summer air. It was about four-thirty, and women's thoughts all over the neighborhood were turning to evening: to cooking dinner and to greeting husbands, to heating water for the predinner baths. The ginkgo leaves directly above her hung motionless, and beneath them Sono sat suspended.

What now? Croquet at the senior citizens' center? At the thought, a flash of protest rose within her. This final period of her life should be more than a pitiful appendage to middle age. Surely it had a significance of its own. If she carried into evening the laws of afternoon—more activities, more people, more duties, beyond all bounds of reason—something crucial would pass her by. Sono did not articulate these ideas but she sensed them, and she sat musing till the ground before her became crisscrossed with the *jizo*'s long shadows.

After that, Sono visited the *jizo* often. She shortened her daily walks and sat under the ginkgo tree instead; her feet were growing heavier lately, a burden to lift off the ground. Now in late summer these deserted grounds were especially pleasant, with the sun setting and cool fingers of breeze beginning to steal across her skin. By the time she dropped onto her bench, the sun would be below the horizon, although some of its warmth still lingered in the stone seat. The sky was then milky green, or sometimes grayish blue, like an oriole egg. Whatever its color, it was illuminated by some mighty light shining behind it, and against this unearthly sky the black branches of the temple yard trees were etched with startling clarity. One tree on a distant hill had no leaves—had it been in a fire? Branches grew straight out from its trunk, naked and curved like the arms of a Balinese dancer: one tip pointing up, the other down, as if poised in exquisite anticipation.

Here she was never lonely.

Sono did occasionally visit the senior citizens' center with her friend from the bathhouse, and she laughed and enjoyed herself. But entering her silent house afterwards was such an adjustment, and each time she sensed anew that these outings—cheerful distractions—did not really match the direction in which her life was headed.

Sono's days now revolved around her evenings in the temple grounds. She ate dinners early and stopped watching the news, in order to have more time to sit on the bench. Here her mind floated freely, from one idea to the next: the wisdom hidden in a certain childhood ditty, or the image of the sky as one giant oriole egg. Seldom in her adult life had Sono had this luxury of completely uninterrupted thought, and as the summer passed, the ease with which she navigated through the world of the abstract increased, even as the strength in her legs diminished. It was like learning to swim: gliding through this new element with growing skill and strength, venturing out into new depths, hastening back to the safety of shore and then, emboldened, heading out again.

There were ten *jizo*. One was much older than the others, a mere lump of rock; moss grew thick as bark over its features and spread its roots in the porous stone. Moss after the rainy season was silky to the touch; to Sono it was like stroking the fur of a small animal. Another *jizo*, better preserved, consisted of two Buddhas standing side by side. These unfortunate twins had been put to death centuries ago; born of opposite sexes, they were assumed to have had sexual contact within the womb. It occurred to Sono, recalling the distaste with which she had once hustled her own twins away, how narrowly the girls would have escaped such a fate in olden times. Yet another *jizo*—illegitimate, according to its stone inscription—had been born dead with an umbilical cord wrapped around its neck.

Birth. Fraught with danger, this transition from one world to the next. Amazing that it succeeded at all. So much could go wrong: women dying in childbirth, fetuses shifting into wrong alignment inside the womb, accidents of cell division—or of social error—growing unchecked for months, only to be destroyed after a pointless waste of hope and energy. And sometimes, for no comprehensible reason, newborns just did not survive; the qualities that had sustained them in the womb proved to be inadequate for the outside world.

Sono thought of those little lives, doomed in their infancy. If she were younger, the very thought of those poor peasant mothers and their babies crying out for each other, understanding nothing, would have twisted her insides with terrible pain. Now, it merely moved her with a vague tender sorrow that was almost pleasurable. Aaa, life . . . so sad, Sono thought, fanning herself with a round paper *uchiwa* as crows cawed their lonely way home over the dark treetops. She felt quite removed from it all. Having little left to lose, little left to desire, had lifted her onto a halcyon mountaintop from which she saw all the sufferings of mankind blending beautifully, like tiny trees, into the landscape below.

And now a new dimension, heavy with infinities of time and space, hung just above reach in the failing light, straining against the glowing membrane of the evening sky. Sono wanted to cup this sky in her palm and gauge the temperature of what lay beyond: cool, surely, like a clear mountain lake. If she could prick the sky with a pin . . .

Did babies in the womb also have premonitions of an outside world? Vibrations, growing stronger as the time approached; then that final period of limbo when familiar walls shrank in places and opened up in others, subtly disturbing the ordered space; amniotic fluid gently shifting in preparation for something incomprehensible. Did babies feel it too—vague anticipations, to be confirmed beyond measure in the shock of birth: chilled air, sounds scraping across a virgin eardrum, hot skin on skin?

Autumn came. The sky fluctuated, in the course of a day, between a high dome of cobalt blue and a flat mottled white. "Autumn skies, women's minds," the old saying went. A smell of burning leaves wafted through every alley, as pungent as incense.

Akimi, Sono's niece, phoned from Aomori Prefecture. "Auntie! The three of us are all flying in next Thursday to help," she said. The equinox was approaching. The family graves needed weeding, altar tablets needed consecrating. "Auntie, you sound like your mind's someplace else lately," she said. "Is that senior citizens' center wearing you out?"

Before they arrived, Sono thought she would walk over to the temple grounds and buy each of them amulets. Amulets made lovely gifts: little silk pouches adorned with tinkling bells, with folded squares of prayer paper inside. And practical as well—people were constantly having to replace them, since their protective capabilities expired after a year. There was no harm in having up-to-date protection, Sono supposed, whether you believed in that sort of thing or not.

She went early the next day. Nan-ben-ji, the largest of the nine temples, opened its little office at eight; the first of the tour buses would not arrive till eight-thirty. The morning air was suffused with a soft lemon yellow, and high up on either side of the flagstone path sunlight streamed through dripping branches—it had rained the night before—bringing down with it the scent of wet pine. The crows were silent, anticipating the tourists; every so often, one cawed.

Somewhere in the distance, a school bell tolled *kinn konn kann konn*.

Sono bought the amulets and then, in no hurry, shuffled down the cold wooden veranda—in slippers, provided at the front gate—to the main prayer room. This room housed the famous life-size Nan-ben-ji Buddha of the Amida sect. Sitting on the floor cushion, she had to look up to see it, and the burnished bronze face, glowing within the shadows of the alcove, looked down to hers.

In the past few months, Sono had grown accustomed to the *jizo*'s smiles: smug, contented smiles of children, eyes closed as if just fed and drifting off to sleep. The more tragic a baby's story, it was said, the happier a smile the stone carver would try to give it. Now, as she gazed up at this bronze face in all its mature, sorrowful powers, Sono saw what a limited nirvana there had been in the *jizo*'s smiles—smiles created for the minds of children, for whom bliss was merely a more comfortable version of their own physical world.

The face above her was neither young nor old, male nor female. It had shed all such characteristics. It had shed all emotion. When she was a child, this had unnerved her: what help could you possibly receive, praying to a smile so disengaged and remote? Now, examining this face, Sono sensed how much of life it held: behind these features had once stirred great joys and griefs. The Nan-ben-ji Buddha smiled down at her now with that same nostalgic sorrow with which she herself had regarded the *jizo,* with that same sense of immense distance.

Sono remembered a time when she had cried with her whole body: dry, ragged sobs heaving up along her spine until she thought they would tear the flesh of her heart. She thought with sorrow of how that heart had changed; something flower-like, each petal exposed to the world, had become a smooth hard husk.

But then, looking up again, Sono recognized that strangely luminous sky of summer twilight, its endless dimensions glowing whitely through the Buddha's muted features. And she was thankful to whoever had left this signpost to testify that he, too, had known this limbo for which there are no words; that through the ages others had known it; and that by her own humble path, she had come to the right place.

Egg-Face

RITSUKO NAKAJIMA was thirty years old, and she had never been on a date. In addition, she had never held a job. The latter might have been acceptable; even in these modern times, many middle-class women in the Kin-nanji district did not work outside the home. But such women were usually married.

"Anything new with that Nakajima girl, the middle one?" some housewife might say while shelling peas with her children on the veranda, or gossiping with neighbors in one of the narrow alleyways leading to the open-air market. There never was. Ritsuko was spotted strolling in the dusk or running the occasional errand at the market; in the mornings, children on their way to school saw her feeding the caged canary on the upstairs balcony. Like some retired person, neighbors said. Like Buddha in a lotus garden.

Wasn't she depressed? Wasn't she desperate? They waylaid her in the alleys: the young housewives applying subtle pressure; the old women probing bluntly, secure in the respect due their age. Ritsuko met their questions (Do you want children someday? What do you do in your free time?) with an indecisive "saaa," a cocked head, and an expression suggesting that such a puzzle had never even crossed her mind before. Comments and advice alike were absorbed with a "haaa" of humble illumination.

"There's no give-and-take," declared old Mrs. Wakame. She was a formidable busybody who ambushed passersby from the comfort of her front stoop, where she lingered on the pretext of watering her dozens of tiny potted flowers. "Talking to that girl is like—" old Mrs. Wakame said, then shook her head and quoted an old saying about a sumo wrestler charging through squares of cotton hung from doorways.

But Ritsuko was not stupid. She was too retiring, even for a girl, but her schoolwork had always been good. Her business degree from Ninjo College would have guaranteed her a job if only this recession, now in its ninth year, had not hit the country just as her class was graduating. Managers had begun to be laid off despite decades of service; quotas for college recruits were slashed below half. Ritsuko, like many in her class, was rejected repeatedly at interviews the summer before March graduation.

Like her classmates, she had waited for the next interviewing season. Up to that point, she did not attract undue attention. But the following summer, when neighbors made polite inquiries of Mrs. Nakajima as to why her daughter was not interviewing—or at least making do with part-time work—they were told that Ritsuko would marry directly from home, bypassing the typical three or four years of premarriage employment. Nine years went by, however, and nothing happened.

Perhaps there was an inheritance? There *was* the house, which was all paid off according to the Tatsumi woman, whose husband worked at Mitsui Bank. But split among three daughters, it wasn't much. Moreover, Mr. Nakajima drew but a modest salary at some little export company in Shiga Prefecture. How much savings could they possibly have after private college tuition for three daughters, not to mention wedding expenses for the eldest? Old Mrs. Wakame had noticed Mrs. Nakajima buying bargain mackerel caught off American shores, as well as low-grade rice from Indonesia and Thailand.

There was little to be gleaned from the other two daughters. The Nakajima sisters, apparently, were not close; Aiko and Chie showed little insight into Ritsuko's mind and even less interest. They at any rate were leading normal lives. Aiko, the eldest, had recently married a confectioner's son and was now living in Gion. Twenty-five-year-old Chie, unmarried and therefore still living at home, had been dating her current boyfriend for five months. She had landed a bank teller job after two years of interviewing; each day she rode the Number 72 bus to and from work, looking like a stewardess in Shinwa Bank's official navy jumper.

"They should have *forced* her to work, for her own good." "Life's just passing her by." "That father should bring home company underlings for dinner. Isn't that how the Fujiwaras met?" Ecstatic approval followed each comment, fanning a glow of well-being that lingered as the housewives went their separate ways. Their ruminations moved in endless circles, like a merry-go-round from which they could disembark at any moment if a better topic came along.

It was out of genuine kindness—as well as curiosity, the kind that drives children to poke sleeping animals—that old Mrs. Wakame phoned Ritsuko's mother. She felt justified in using the telephone, because this time, unlike other outdoor occasions when Mrs. Nakajima had managed to slip away, she had a legitimate favor to bestow. This sense of the upper hand made old Mrs. Wakame's voice expansive. A young man, she told Mrs. Nakajima, a former student of her retired husband, was interested in marriage. Should she act as matchmaker and set up a meeting?

There was a brief silence.

"That is very kind," Mrs. Nakajima said with dignity. "We accept."

Mrs. Nakajima herself had married through a matchmaker, but that was decades ago; nowadays, love marriages were prevalent. As a result, Ritsuko had received only one other matchmaking offer, five years ago, involving an elementary-school principal with forty-three years to Ritsuko's twenty-five. Trusting in future offers, Mrs. Nakajima had declined without even setting up a meeting. "A middle-aged man! How could I do that to a young girl?" she had said. "It would just crush her spirit."

"What spirit?" said her youngest daughter, Chie. That scornful remark had hurt Mrs. Nakajima deeply, for of her three daughters Ritsuko resembled her mother the most.

Today, Mrs. Nakajima and Ritsuko sat at the kitchen table in the awkward aftermath of old Mrs. Wakame's phone call. It was about four o'clock, and Mr. Nakajima and Chie were still at work. Granny was home—she sat upstairs all day, coming down only for meals—but by unspoken assent, they made no move to go to her with the news.

A breeze wafted in through the open window, bringing with it the aggressive smell of fresh grass. Since the last rain, weeds had invaded the neighborhood, appearing overnight, in startling hues of neon, through cracks in the asphalt, from under ceramic roof tiles, even within the stone lanterns in the garden. The garden itself, cut off from the western sun by a high bamboo fence, now lay in deepening shadow.

Also drifting in on the breeze, from the direction of Asahi Middle School, came the synchronized shouts—"Fight! Fight! Fight!"—of the baseball team running laps. It was April again, the start of another new school year.

Instinctively Mrs. Nakajima considered closing the window, turning on the little radio that was permanently set, at cozy low volume, to the easy-listening station. For the shouts were a disturbing reminder that for the past nine years, while Ritsuko's life ground to a halt, mindless toddlers had been transforming into young adults whose voices now rose with strength and promise. Aaa, each new spring came so quickly! . . . As if the rest of the world followed a different clock.

But the phone call changed things. Suddenly the air in the kitchen, which still smelled faintly of this morning's prayer incense, altered—attuning itself to that elusive forward momentum of the outside world. For the first time, Mrs. Nakajima dared to hope her daughter's destiny could be saved, like a pan snatched from a stove in the nick of time.

With a sharp, anxious sigh, Mrs. Nakajima pushed herself up from the low table. Ritsuko, idly prying off the label from a jar of salted plums, glanced up in mild puzzlement.

"That jar's so low already," Mrs. Nakajima said by way of explanation.

"I can buy another jar," Ritsuko offered. "I'll take my bicycle." She ran errands for everyone in the family, which was only fair since she wasn't working. That had been Mrs. Nakajima's job for many years. She had not minded it for herself, but it smote her to see the same affable subservience in her daughter.

According to the résumé, Kanzo Funaba was twenty-eight years old—Ritsuko's junior by two years. He had a business degree from Noraku University, where old Mr. Wakame had taught (hardly an elite school but a good one), and he held a position as assistant manager at a merchandising company called Sabin Kogyo. Two photographs were enclosed with the résumé, casual outdoor shots: Kanzo in a wet suit, sitting on the beach and gazing pensively out over the waters of Kobe Bay; Kanzo in a Nike T-shirt, triumphantly holding aloft a small mackerel on a line.

"His hobbies," Mr. Nakajima read over the gentle clacking of chopsticks at the dinner table, "are scuba diving, sailing, dirt biking, and deep-sea fishing."

"Hehhhh!" Around the table, there was an exhaling of exaggerated awe.

"Expensive hobbies," remarked Granny. She held out the photographs at arm's length, gripping the rim of her eyeglasses with a free hand as if it were a telescope. She noted with a quickening of interest—nothing much, after all, ever happened upstairs—that this boy was better-looking than Ritsuko.

The entire discussion had an air of unreality. Over the years, it had been an unspoken rule to spare Ritsuko any reminder of her situation; tonight, however, the practical necessities of Mrs. Wakame's offer unleashed in the family a heady tingle.

Chie, born in the year of the tiger, had just had an exhausting day at the bank. This was not the life she had envisioned for herself. Her feet ached. One of these days her ankles would swell up like some old matron's. And tomorrow would be no better, nor the day after that. Oh, what was the point of struggling and coming home spent, only to see Big Sister smiling and doing nothing, *not a single thing,* and getting everyone's sympathy besides? Granny actually gave her spending money out of her pension because "the poor girl has no income of her own." And now a prospective husband was dropped into her lap, a better catch than Chie's own boyfriend at the office. It was not to be borne.

"Let's hope you can keep up with him," she said to her big sister.

Ritsuko cocked her head in her usual evasive way but said nothing.

Mrs. Nakajima waved away Chie's remark with an airy gesture that was at odds with the fierce, helpless glance she shot in her youngest daughter's direction. "Men don't care about that kind of thing, do they, Papa?" she said. Mr. Nakajima grunted, still staring at the résumé. Chie chewed stonily. Her red fingernail polish gleamed under the electric light.

"Well, well," Granny said heartily, "that Wakame woman has once again outdone herself."

There had been a time, several years ago, when Chie had insisted on knowing all the details of her mother's courtship. "Saa," Mrs. Nakajima had told her, "we dated for three months. He used to visit me once a week on his way home from work. I remember we took lovely walks in the dusk."

"Did you flirt with each other?" Chie asked. It had caught her mother off guard. Neither of her other daughters had asked such a bald question.

"Of course not!" Mrs. Nakajima said. "It was nothing like that." The impact of her words, now beyond retrieval, spread out in slow motion to fill the moment.

"He never even took you downtown?" Chie was referring to those chic tearooms where, since before the war, young men in love were known to take their dates.

"I don't recall," Mrs. Nakajima had said shortly. She met Chie's level gaze and felt, for a brief instant, a stab of dislike. "We preferred eating pork buns or fried noodles at one of the local places."

Tonight at the dinner table, Mr. Nakajima expounded on Kanzo Funaba's workplace. He had heard good things about Sabin Kogyo. Despite this long recession plaguing the country, Sabin Kogyo had remained stable: its asset-liability ratio was excellent, and the yearly decline of its annual gross revenue was milder than those of most of its counterparts in the industry. The family fell silent before these indisputable statistics.

"It might really happen, ne!" Mrs. Nakajima whispered to her husband later that night, as they lay down to sleep on their separate futons.

"Nnn, it might!" he replied.

"Kobe's not far," Mrs. Nakajima said. "She can come visit us on the train." They stared up into the dark, thinking. Mrs. Nakajima had never had a boyfriend before her marriage. Mr. Nakajima had dated sporadically, his crowning achievement being a one-night sexual encounter with a barmaid at the establishment he and his co-workers frequented after work. They had no advice to pass on to Ritsuko. They did not fully comprehend how they themselves had become linked together; they merely hoped Ritsuko would grow into marriage as they had—in the same mysterious way she had learned to crawl, then later to walk.

Old Mrs. Wakame was feeling the first stirrings of doubt. Just this afternoon she had met Kanzo Funaba and his parents for the first time—something she should have done before approaching the Nakajimas, but at the time she had not been able to wait. A silent young man, she reported to the housewives standing about her front stoop. But not shy. Just silent. . . .

What old Mrs. Wakame did not mention was how much this young man reminded her of her own teenage grandson, who had declared, when he was six, "Granny, I love you better than anybody else." That moment still burned in her chest, but with pain now. For lately, whenever his parents brought him to visit, he sat before the television, distant and bored. Every so often, he would condescend to utter a strained little "hohhh" at her best offerings of gossip. Only when he talked to his own friends—Mrs. Wakame had overheard him using her hallway phone—did his voice take on the animated and confidential tones he had once used with her. This young man Kanzo Funaba exuded the same air as her grandson.

"Sohh—" said one woman, nodding deeply. "Parents are pressuring him."

He'll liven up, Mrs. Wakame assured them, once he meets Ritsuko.

The problem, according to one of the housewives, was that matchmaking was not what it had once been. Men who used it these days no longer understood the subtle difference between evaluating an arranged-marriage prospect versus a love-match prospect. This boy Kanzo, with his fancy hobbies (neighbors had seen photos; old Mrs. Wakame had made copies), seemed typical of a new breed that confused matchmakers with dating services.

"Soh soh," someone else said, "they grow up watching *actresses* on television."

A Mrs. Konishi, whose own daughter had just gotten engaged (a love match), made a pretty moue of concern. Poor Ritsuko, she said. In the old days she would have been just fine. Ritsuko had the qualities of an ideal wife: gentleness, deference, domesticity. Plus a college degree.

Eighty-two-year-old Mrs. Tori, bowed over a trembling cane, lifted her head. Even in our day, she said querulously, men liked women who could at least hold up their own end of a conversation.

⁓⁓

Aiko, Mrs. Nakajima's eldest daughter, came over from Gion on the local bus. It was Thursday. Ritsuko's date was set for Saturday afternoon.

"I don't understand," Aiko said to her mother, who had been waiting for her outside in the alley. "Chie knows makeup as well as I do. Plus she *lives* here."

"It isn't fitting," Mrs. Nakajima whispered, glancing toward the house, "for younger sisters to be teaching older sisters. Besides . . ." She lifted her head, its home-permed waves webbed with white hairs, and looked up at her tall daughter. "Besides, Chie has the wrong attitude." Her haggard expression gave Aiko, who had seen little of her family since her own recent wedding, an eerie glimpse of her mother in old age.

In the dining room, which boasted the best natural light, Aiko now spread out the contents of her plastic makeup pouch onto the large low table. "We'll just do one side of your face," she told her little sister, "so you can see the difference."

"Haaa . . . ," Ritsuko agreed, nodding but not venturing to touch anything. Mrs. Nakajima retired to the kitchen in high spirits, humming a Strauss waltz.

As children, Aiko and Ritsuko had played together at this table when Aiko's more lively neighborhood friends were unavailable, for the sisters were close in age, whereas Chie was five years behind. Today Aiko recalled an early memory: a silent house, rain making pinpricks of sound on the broad hydrangea leaves in the garden. In the bracken-filtered light, she and Ritsuko had drawn pictures or gazed out the window. *Jikkuri-gata,* their mother had teased: characters of contemplation. Time passed. They were—in her memory—silent: mindless, timeless, knowing they were provided for, vaguely registering the faint clatter of the outside world. Dinner noises in the kitchen . . . an ambulance siren in the distance . . .

Ritsuko had managed to remain in that world. Aiko thought of what awaited her back at home: laundry, cooking, wrapping tea sweets for tomorrow's customers, the already faded romance with her husband, the perpetual polite tension of living among in-laws. She sat on an unfamiliar red floor cushion that must have been purchased after she moved away, and she thought how quickly she had become a visitor in her own home.

Ritsuko, with self-conscious care, was dabbing her face with a damp foundation sponge. "Egg-Face," some boy had once called her in fourth grade, and the name had stuck for the remainder of her elementary-school years. Her mother would pacify her ("An oval face is a sign of beauty! White skin is better than dark!"), while Granny, skilled at self-promotion, remarked, "At least she takes after me in the skin area." In truth there was a certain quality to Ritsuko's cheekbones, packed high like an Eskimo's, which lent to her face the suggestion of a blank shell. Her other features, overshadowed by this denseness of bone, appeared shrunken in contrast. The children in their unwitting astuteness had caught her essence: that bland surface of her personality which allowed, with minimal effort, deflection of any attack.

"Now some blush." Aiko handed Ritsuko the oversize brush. "Put on as much as you're comfortable with. No, right here. The round part of your cheek." Ritsuko touched the tip of the brush to her skin: once, then twice.

"More than *that*!" Aiko's voice rose in exasperation. She flicked her own wrist rapidly, suggesting many, many more strokes.

"Ara!" Ritsuko breathed as a soft stain of pink, barely visible, bloomed on her cheek. "It's pretty." Then, apparently embarrassed by this outburst, she lowered her gaze to the blush compact in her lap. She shut it with a tiny click.

Their mother came in to view the result: a job worthy of the Shiseido ads, in subtle tones of gray and peach. Mrs. Nakajima examined it with a look of wonder; she herself had never gone beyond liquid foundation, adding red lipstick only when she went out. "Lovely," she said, "just lovely. Aren't you glad, Ritsuko-chan?" Ritsuko, with an obliging laugh, nodded. "Look at yourself in the mirror!" her mother said, steering her around to face the mirror and looking over her shoulder.

Mrs. Nakajima, peering at Ritsuko's flushed face in the mirror, understood that a change had taken place. In her daughter's eyes was a look she had seen in alley cats, when they warily approached a proffered treat. It was a look terrible and bottomless in its hope. Mrs. Nakajima's belly shifted in unease, as if her body knew something she did not.

Unsure what to make of this, Mrs. Nakajima put it from her mind. The three of them went upstairs to show Granny. She was hunched over on a floor cushion, watching sumo on television. "There—which side of her face looks better?" Aiko demanded, pushing Ritsuko forward.

"Maaa, what an improvement!" cried the old lady, looking up and clapping her hands. "That side, definitely. Look how dewy and white the skin is!"

No one spoke.

"*Granny!*" said Aiko. Her voice became loud and slow even though there was nothing wrong with Granny's hearing. "We didn't even *do* that side. We did the *other* side." She exchanged a wry glance with her mother. Even Ritsuko gave a little smile, tucking her hair behind one ear.

After they had gone, Granny turned back to her little television set. She could no longer concentrate on the sumo match; she still seemed to hear Aiko's muffled laughter drifting up the stairs. Maa, so what if her eyesight was no longer perfect? In her own day, at least, she had been a great beauty. Upslanted eyes ("exquisite, like bamboo leaves," someone had said), a face compared with the one in that famous Tondai lithograph, a long shapely neck that was the envy of her village. She had held sway over a dozen eligible suitors, eventually marrying into a professor's family despite her own lack of education. How dare they forget it! Her daughter-in-law, her granddaughters—for all their pitiful fuss over face paint—had nothing to work with. Ridiculous bumpkins! Oh, youth and insolence would leave them soon enough. A nervous tic began throbbing under her left eye.

"How did it go, do you think?" Mrs. Nakajima whispered for the second time to old Mrs. Wakame, who was sitting beside her on the homebound train. "Did he like her, do you think? Will he ask to meet her again?" Ritsuko was sitting three seats ahead, out of earshot.

The lunch date had taken place at a restaurant called Miyagi, whose sushi turned out to be, befitting its seaside location, of uncommonly good quality. Old Mrs. Wakame loved sushi, especially the *kampachi,* which she and her husband could now rarely afford on his pension. But her matchmaking duties came first, so for the first half of the date she delayed eating, chatting instead about everything from weather to chrysanthemums. The auspicious cuisine, as well as the pleasant conversation (mostly among the four parents, although this was to be expected), erased the uneasiness of her earlier meeting with Kanzo.

It was further into the lunch, after they had covered jobs and hobbies (Ritsuko's hobbies were walking and reading) and the table's energy was flagging from the generous portions of salmon and *hamachi* and eel and squid, that Kanzo began amusing himself with questions of his own. "Ritsuko-san, what is your favorite color?" he asked, tapping his cigarette over an ashtray. "Ritsuko-san, what is your favorite animal?"

Old Mrs. Wakame threw him an uncertain glance, but his handsome face looked reassuring, full of the grave manly concern that was so attractive in samurai dramas. And Ritsuko was holding her own so well, answering each question correctly after a long thoughtful pause, although at times she did present her answers with unnecessary bows that were quick and clumsy, like a child's. So Mrs. Wakame paid them little heed. Hunching over her lacquered box, she applied herself singlemindedly to the sushi she had been waiting for, narrowing her eyes in pleasure as the freshly ground wasabi warmed her sinuses.

She suddenly came to. Kanzo's question was ringing in her ears: "Ritsuko-san, what do you want most in life?" The table was silent, save for the steady clinks of ice in the men's whiskey glasses. Kanzo's mother, a fashionably dressed woman, glanced at her watch.

"Saaa—" With all eyes upon her, Ritsuko cocked her head.

"We all want the same thing, don't we," Mrs. Nakajima

broke in, nodding at her daughter as if in agreement. "A long healthy life, happiness . . ."

With a small predatory smile, Kanzo Funaba exhaled cigarette smoke toward the ceiling.

Recalling this now, old Mrs. Wakame sighed and shifted position on her train seat. "Saaa, it went well enough, don't you think?" she said to Ritsuko's mother. "Who can predict?" she added.

They both fell silent, sipping Morinaga Orange Drink from slender cans around which they had wrapped their handkerchiefs.

The train rattled along the tracks and the city spread out below them: modern high-rises crowding out old buildings of wood and tile, balconies and verandas bedecked with futons hung out to air. The spring air was translucent with smog. All the soot expelled during the day—all the soot expelled during this long depression—was falling back down to earth, the sediment floating in the busy streets. Late-afternoon sunlight slanted through it, creating an amber viscosity in which the traffic below would eventually still.

Old Mrs. Wakame stood up to roll down the shade, and her eye fell upon a travel poster displayed above the window: a promotion for some resort showing, in brilliant colors, a lone crane flying over snowfields. It brought to mind the television program she had seen last night, an NHK dramatization of the Crane Maiden legend: a crane, rescued from a trap by an old weaver, returns to him disguised as a beautiful maiden. This role was played by the lovely Junji Mariko in a rare appearance. The credits said so, at any rate, but who could really tell? Her face was averted from the camera, shielded by a fall of glossy hair. She would weave him wondrous silks free of charge, she murmured, as long as he promised never to watch her in the process. "You mustn't peek," she implored. "I couldn't bear for you to learn the secret of my weaving."

Something about that graceful turning away of the head— so old-fashioned, and now extinct—had touched old Mrs. Wakame deeply. And when the weaver, overcome by curiosity, finally peeked through a crack in the shoji screen ("Is that actor Mori Daiji?" asked her husband, exhaling a cloud of cigarette smoke. "Maaa, he's certainly aged"), Mrs. Wakame had uttered a shrill cry of awful nameless regret. She had felt silly afterwards. For everyone knew what he would see: a crane, half-plucked and grotesque, feeding its own feathers into the loom . . .

What this had to do with anything, Mrs. Wakame did not know. Again, she shifted position on the plush seat. Images flashed into her mind of Ritsuko at the lunch table: lipstick smeared on her front tooth, trembling hands with red-painted fingernails bitten to the quick. "I would like children," she had said, as smoke from Kanzo's ashtray rose up between them. "I have always wanted children." Remorse hit old Mrs. Wakame like a wave, and she lowered her Morinaga Orange Drink onto the windowsill.

The Way Love Works

I WAS THIRTEEN when my mother and I flew back to Japan on what, unbeknownst to us, would be our final visit together. I was eager, after a five-year absence and eleven hours of flying, to see our family. But when we emerged from airport customs into the path of countless searching eyes, it took some moments to spot them. They were standing shoulder to shoulder, pressed up against the rails: Grandma, Aunt Miho, Uncle Koku, my cousins, Grandpa Ichiro with his special-occasion beret. A fraction of a second later, I felt Mother's carry-on bag swipe my arm as she rushed past me toward her mother.

The rest of us watched, keeping such a respectful distance from Mother and Grandma that several travelers used the space as a pathway, momentarily blocking them from our sight. The two women faced each other and gripped hands, their knuckles white. Being Japanese, that was all they did, but with such trembling intensity, like lovers, that I almost shriveled with embarrassment.

Mother and Grandma stayed indoors during the entire month of our visit, chatting away with hardly a break. They paused only out of politeness to others: my aunt Miho, who lived ten blocks away; Grandpa Ichiro, asking vague questions about America (do they eat bread at every meal?); phone calls; visitors. "I'm *bored*!" I said. "Can't I go swimming? Can't I go to Summer Haunted House?"

"Go with your cousins," they suggested. "We'll just stay here." They waved good-bye from the doorway as Aunt Miho, with us four children in tow, headed down the alley to the bus stop under the glaring summer sun. When we reached the corner and looked back for a final wave, the two of them were bending over some potted bonsai trees, already engrossed in conversation. They saw us, quickly straightened, and waved in unison.

I grew familiar with the ebb and flow of their talk. In the mornings—while cooking breakfast, washing up, walking to the open-air market—it was bright and animated, bubbling over with bits of gossip, or additions to previous conversations, which had risen to the surface of their memories during sleep. Afternoons, in the lull between lunch and four o'clock (when the local bathhouse opened), gave rise to more sustained, philosophical topics. Since Grandpa Ichiro took his nap then, it was also a good time for whispered confidences. "Nobody knows this except you," I heard Grandma say many times. They sometimes discussed mysterious financial issues: in the trash can I found scratch paper with hastily scrawled calculations using multiplication and long division.

I hadn't caught such nuances when I was eight; I now watched these comings and goings with avid foreign eyes. But even more fascinating than these allegiances was the change in my mother.

Five years earlier, my mother, my Caucasian father, and I had sold our home in Japan and moved to a small logging town in Northern California, surrounded by miles of walnut and plum orchards. "Did you meet up with your husband when he was in the service?" Americans always asked Mother. She hated that question. "Don't these people *think*?" she fumed in private. "Do they even realize what they're insinuating?"

"No . . . he was never in the service . . . ," she always replied, as if in apology. "I have never had the *honor* of meeting a service man."

"Oh, honey," the neighbor women told me, "your momma's just *precious*!"

Back in America, Mother spoke English: heavily accented and sometimes halting, but always grammatically correct. When she felt lighthearted, she broke into Japanese with me. For the most part, however, she was a severe disciplinarian. She never lounged. She never snacked between meals. She scrubbed, gardened, hand-laundered, even in cold weather when the skin on her fingertips split open in raw cracks. She pulled back her hair, which was glossy even though she used nothing on it but Johnson's Baby Shampoo, into a French twist. Only occasionally at bedtime would I see it undone at shoulder length, making her face look unformed and girlish.

But here in Japan, she gossiped, giggled, teased. Once or

twice I caught her watching me with that eager, open look of someone in love. While Grandma made the miso soup for breakfast, Mother stood before the cupboard and nibbled on red bean cakes, beckoning for me to join her. I did, warily.

"Koraa!" Grandma scolded, coming in from the kitchen with the tray.

"But, Mama," Mother protested in a loud voice, with a conspiratorial glance at me, "these taste so *good* . . . Meri-chan and I are so *hungry* . . ."

I remember thinking that each language carried its own aura, its own mood, and that people fell under its spell.

"I suppose it's only courteous," Mother said, "to visit Miho's house in return. After all, she's always coming over here."

"Yes, you're absolutely right," Grandma said. "But hurry back."

"How come Grandma likes you best?" I asked my mother as the two of us walked toward Aunt Miho's house.

She laughed it off with her new playful air. "Saa, I happen to have a lot of special qualities," she said. "I'm irreplaceable."

Aunt Miho was young and pretty; I had often fantasized about having her for a big sister. She and Mother were half sisters, due to some family complication I grasped only dimly at the time. Aunt Miho's father was Grandpa Ichiro. Mother's father—my own true grandfather—was long dead.

"How's your visit so far?" Aunt Miho asked me at the lunch table. "Are you having lots of fun?" Her intonation was gentle and courteous, like that of a JAL stewardess, with each word hanging in perfect balance.

"Yes, Auntie," I said.

"Hajime said he heard lots of laughing the other night," she said, "when he passed by your place on his way home from work." We all looked at Aunt Miho's husband, who glanced up, discomfited, from his plate of skewered miso dumplings.

"Oh—there must have been something funny on TV," Mother said. *"The Nishikawa Gang,* probably. Do you ever watch it? That is a *hilarious* show."

"Soh, it *is*!" I assured Aunt Miho. "Grandma was saying she hasn't laughed like this in years!"

"Oh," said Aunt Miho. "How nice."

On the tatami floor, right under the low table where we all sat, I noticed a leather-bound Bible. By overhearing—or eaves-dropping—I knew that Aunt Miho had turned Christian during our absence. I lifted the book out into the open; Mother frowned and jerked her head no.

I put the book back.

"You can look at that anytime you like," said Aunt Miho in her serene voice. "It's filled with strange and wonderful stories. About loving without limits. Despite anything others might do."

"Even if they're *murderers*?" I asked. Mother shot me a cold glance.

Aunt Miho smiled. "There is no power," she said, "greater than forgiveness." Aunt Miho's husband, a quiet man, got up and went to the bathroom.

"A *hilarious* show . . . ," murmured six-year-old Mikiko. I glanced over at my three small cousins, sitting quietly at the far end of the table. With what must have been ease of habit, they had filled their glasses with exactly four ice cubes each and lined them up, side by side, on the table. They peered, unblinking, as their mother poured the orange Fanta, the children hunching down at the low table so as to be eye-level with the glasses, thus ensuring that no sibling got a milliliter more than the others.

"Did you see them with those drinking glasses?" Mother said on our way home. "If you had brothers and sisters, that's what you'd be doing. See how lucky you are, being an only child?"

I did. I would undoubtedly lose out in a competition of favorites. With a flush of shame, I remembered my behavior back home: how I constantly contradicted Mother in an exasperated tone, taking advantage of her ineptness in what, for her, was a foreign country.

But my behavior had changed since our arrival; the language also cast its spell over me. I was fluent in Japanese—it was my first language—but since our move to America, my vocabulary had stayed at a fourth-grade level. So in Japan my speech, even my thoughts, reverted from those of a cocky teenager to those of the more innocent, dependent child I had been five years ago. Here I was no longer capable of arguing with the contemptuous finesse I used back home. Here I was at a loss.

"But don't worry, Meri-chan," my mother said. "I could never have feelings for any other child but you." I was still unused to *chan,* that tender diminutive to a little girl's name for which English has no equivalent. Hearing such words, after all those years in America, made my throat grow tight. I could not have talked back, even if I had the words.

Mother took advantage of my weakened state. She slipped

her hand into mine, a big girl like me, right in public. During the course of our stay, she would do this several times: tentatively at first, then with increasing confidence as the month wore on. This would not last once we flew home; the mere act of standing on American soil would destroy that precarious balance.

Now Mother strode along, leading the way; among the local Japanese, she seemed much taller than her five feet three inches. Near the steps of Heibuchi Shrine, we ran into Mr. Inoue, her former high school principal. "I hope you take after your mother," he told me. "She was the first girl from the Ueno district to pass Kyoto University entrance exams." I stood with my hand damp and unmoving in my mother's, still bashful from our newfound intimacy. I watched the old man bowing with slow, ceremonious respect. I heard their polite conversation, replete with advanced verb conjugations. My mother's sentences flowed sinuously, with nuances of silver and light, like a strong fish gliding through the Kamo River.

The next day, I asked Mother whom she loved best in the world.

"My mother, of course," she replied. We were coming home from the open-air market. She was walking ahead of me; the alley was too narrow for the two of us to walk abreast. Dappled shadows jerked and bobbed on the back of her parasol.

"And my dad?"

"He's number two."

"Who's number three?"

"You! Of course." But I suspected, with a flash of intuition, that I was a very close third, probably even a tie for second. Not that I deserved it. I was an unpleasant teenager, whereas my father was a good, kind man. Nonetheless I belonged to this Japanese world, whose language and blood ties gave my mother such radiant power, in a way my American father never could.

"Who's number four?" I asked, assured of my good status. "Who's number five?" Too late. Mother's thoughts had drifted somewhere else.

"When you come first in someone's heart," she said, "when you feel the magnitude of another person's love for you . . ." Her gait slowed, along with her speech. "You become a different person. I mean, something physically changes inside of you." Her voice choked up behind the parasol and I hoped she was not going to cry. "I want you to know that feeling," she said. "Because it'll sustain you, all your life. Life . . . life can get so hard."

So hard . . . Was she referring to my behavior back home? Guilty and defensive, I trailed my fingers along a low adobe wall in nonchalant fashion, over its braille of pebbles and straw. A smell of earth, intensified by midsummer heat, wafted toward me.

My relationship with my mother was not a bad one, by normal standards. I understand this now. But back then, the only yardstick either of us had was the bond between Mother and Grandma; it must have been a disappointment to my mother, as it was to me that summer, that we could not replicate it.

"You're Grandma's favorite grandchild," my mother said eventually in a recovered voice.

"Really?" I said, gratified. That question had been next on my agenda.

"Don't flatter yourself," she said, "that it's on your own merits. Not yet. It's because you're my child. You reach her through me. Remember that."

"Okay," I agreed. The *k'sha k'sha* of gravel was loud beneath our sandals. The buzz of late-afternoon traffic floated over from Shimbonmachi Boulevard, several blocks down.

"You and I are lucky," Mother said. "Some people never come first." I thought of Aunt Miho, how she had turned back at the corner to wave.

In silence we entered the shade of a large ginkgo tree, which leaned out over the adobe wall into the alley. Its fan-shaped leaves, dangling from thin stems, fluttered and trembled.

Mother stopped walking and lowered her parasol, turning her head this way and that. The *meeeeee* of cicadas was directly overhead now, sharpened from a mass drone into the loud rings of specific creatures; each with a different pitch, a different location among the branches.

"Take a good look around, Meri-chan," she said, attempting to make a sweeping gesture with an arm weighed down by a plastic bag full of daikon radishes and lotus roots. "This alley hasn't changed a bit since I was a girl. It's still got the *feel* this whole city used to have, once."

I looked. My eyes, still accustomed to California sun, registered this new light of a foreign latitude: a hushed gold approaching amber, angling across the alley in dust-moted shafts as if through old stained glass. An aged world. I pictured Mother playing here decades ago, to the drone of cicadas and the occasional *ting* of a wind chime: countless quiet afternoons, their secrets lost to the next generation.

"Ara maa!" Mother said regretfully. "Somebody's gone and replaced their slatted wooden doors with that all-weather metal kind."

Aunt Miho visited us frequently. Several times, when the grown-ups were reminiscing about old times and everyone sat basking in familial warmth and intimacy, she took the opportunity to slip in something about Love or the Lord. Our laughter trailed away, and we fell silent as she talked: Mother, nodding with restless eyes (when did Miho start using that *voice,* she said in private), Grandma, her gaze averted with a certain sorrowful submission.

Aunt Miho targeted Grandma and Mother. Grandpa Ichiro was spared; he was losing his hearing, usually off in a world of his own. I too was excused, since my vocabulary was insufficient for grasping the finer points of Christian theory. "Wait, what does that word mean?" I demanded anyway at crucial moments. "Wait, wait! What does it *mean?*"

In the late afternoons, I overheard Grandma and Mother talking. "Childhood insecurities," Mother whispered.

Grandma sighed. "It's all my fault," she said.

"It is *not* your fault!" Mother said.

It came to a head one week before our departure. My cousin, six-year-old Mikiko, came into the kitchen, where Grandma and Mother and I were sitting. "Mama says you don't want to come with us to Heaven," she accused, clasping her tiny arms around Grandma's knees and gazing up at her with moist, reproachful eyes. "Ne, is that true?"

"Miki-chan, it's very complicated," Grandma said.

"How come you aren't coming to Heaven with us? Don't you want to be with us?"

"Ara maa . . . ," Grandma protested, and stood helplessly stroking Mikiko's head over and over.

Mother's lips took on a compressed look I knew well. I followed as she strode down the hall to the room where Aunt Miho was watching a cooking show on television. Mother slid shut the shoji panel with a *pang* behind her. I listened from the hallway, on the other side of the panel.

"Raise your child any way you want, but don't you dare use her that way against my mother." My mother's voice was barely audible. "Can't you *realize,* how much pain she's had in her life?" she said. "How many times, since we were children, have I *pleaded* with you to protect her in my absence?

"And speaking bluntly," Mother continued, "what you want from our mother is impossible. *My* father's in Buddhist heaven, waiting for her. And when she dies, I'll be at the temple chanting sutras for *her.* First-year anniversary, third, seventh, thirteenth, thirty-third, fiftieth! For the rest of my life. Even if I burn in your Christian Hell for it!"

Her wrath was magnificent and primal. At that moment, it didn't even occur to me to feel sorry for Aunt Miho. I was swept up in an unexpected sense of vindication as well as a powerful loyalty to our trio. Over the following week, I was to sit before the vanity mirror and practice pressing my lips together the way Mother had. I would watch my face, with its pointy Caucasian features, become transformed with authority and passion. It would be many years before I felt the poignancy of Mother's belligerent, childlike loyalty, with which she shielded Grandma from the others.

Mother's voice now softened, for Aunt Miho was crying. "Someday," she said, "you'll understand, Miho. You'll understand, the way love works."

Even then, I sensed that my grandfather—not Grandpa Ichiro but my true grandfather—was a key catalyst in our family relations. That summer, for the first time, I was shown my grandfather Yasunari's photograph album, concealed in a dresser among layers of folded winter kimonos. "Now remember," Grandma and Mother told me, "this is just among us. The rest of them wouldn't like it if they knew. Grandpa Ichiro either. Especially Grandpa Ichiro!" The album was bound in ugly brownish cloth which, according to Grandma, was once a beautiful indigo; it had matching brown tassels that were still dark blue in their centers. I was discouraged from touching it. Grandma and Mother turned the pages, with hands smelling of lemony dishwashing soap.

Mother never knew her father; she was only five when Yasunari died in the war. Throughout her childhood she, too, had been shown this album, during stolen moments when the others were away. It was hard to believe this young man in the black-and-white photographs, her own true father, was as much a stranger to her as he was to me. Yasunari was handsome, like a movie star, with fine molded features and eyes like elegant brushstrokes.

"We were happy, very happy," Grandma told me. "Yasunari-san loved children. Every minute he had free, he was carrying your mother. Walking around, always holding her in one arm."

"I think I remember being held by him," Mother said.

"When he finally set your mother down, she'd cry. And keep on crying. Your mother, even back then, she could read people. And sure enough, he'd laugh and pick her back up. She even sat on his lap at dinnertime."

I learned the rest of this story when I was nineteen, after Mother's sudden death from mitral valve failure. Holding an adult conversation with my grandmother was an adjustment; I was so used to being the nonessential part of a threesome. But in the wake of Mother's death, we took on new roles: she as surrogate mother, I as surrogate daughter. In this new capacity we spent hours discovering each other, with all the obsessions and raised hopes of a courtship.

Before the war, Grandma told me, Yasunari was a highly paid executive in the import-export business. When he died, he left young Grandma with a sizable inheritance. But her in-laws, determined to keep Yasunari's money in the family, pressured her into marrying his elder brother Ichiro. Family obligation, they argued. A father for the child. Protection from wartime dangers.

Ichiro was a dandy. Despite the grinding poverty of those war years, he insisted on sporting an ascot and not a tie. A social creature, popular with both men and women, he drank with a fast set and then, flushed with sake, shook hands on tenuous business deals. In a short time he had gone through much of his younger brother's inheritance. In contrast to his outward persona, Ichiro was surly at home, irritable and quick to find blame for the smallest things.

Even today, more than a decade after Mother's death, Grandma revisits this as she and I sit alone, looking through

Yasunari's album. She speaks in a whisper, the same whisper she once used with Mother in late afternoons, even though Grandpa Ichiro is dead now and we two have the house to ourselves.

Many nights, Grandma tells me, she stood at the kitchen window while everyone slept, gazing at the moon caught among pine branches. Many nights she dreamed the same dream: Yasunari was outside in the night, standing silent in the alley. She could not see him, but she knew, as one does in dreams, that he was wearing a white suit like that of a Cuban musician.

"Take me with you! Please! Don't leave me here!" she screamed after him in the dream, and woke to the sound of her own moaning.

Grandma went on to bear two children by Grandpa Ichiro: my uncle Koku, then my aunt Miho. In old photographs little Koku and Miho are always out in front, their beaming, gap-toothed faces playing up to the camera; although Grandpa is out of the picture, one senses his presence behind the lens, directing jokes to his favorites. Grandma stands off to the back, and Mother does too, her torso turned toward her mother in an oddly protective stance.

In this atmosphere, Mother's social awareness developed early. She massaged her mother's shoulders when no one was looking. She secretly threatened her half siblings when they misbehaved. She became a model student as well as a model daughter, thus depriving Grandpa Ichiro of any excuse to harass Grandma on her account.

In my mother, Grandma found an outlet for all the ardent romantic love she had felt for Yasunari. This child, she thought, is all I have left: of his genes, of his loyal, solicitous nature. Often Grandma left her chores and hurried over to the neighborhood playground where, using sleight of hand, she would slip a treat into Mother's pocket: a bit of baked potato in winter, to keep her warm; in hot weather, a tiny salted rice ball with a pinch of sour plum at its center. This was during the postwar days, in the midst of food rationing.

There just wasn't enough, she tells me now, for the other children.

Aunt Miho dropped by last week during O-bon, the Week of the Dead, bringing one of those seven-thousand-yen gift melons that come in their own box. She sat alone at the dining room table, sipping cold wheat tea. All afternoon we had visitors: friends of Mother, dead thirteen years now; friends of Grandpa Ichiro, dead three years. They all trooped past her into the altar room, bowing politely as they passed. Aunt Miho listened from the dining room as they chanted sutras at the family altar and struck the miniature gong. Christians cannot acknowledge Buddhist holidays, much less pay homage to their ancestors.

I put the melon on a dish and took it to the altar room, placing it on the slide-out shelf among a clutter of orchids and boxed pastries. "Mother and Grandpa Ichiro used to love those melons," I told her, coming back into the dining room. "Auntie, you're the only one who remembered."

She smiled, with a warmth that her daughters rarely show me. She is still pretty. She now wears her hair swept back in a French twist, a style similar to my mother's.

This afternoon, Grandma and I discuss Aunt Miho's new hairstyle as we stroll to the open-air market to buy *hiramasa* sushi for supper. Our conversation has the same familiar rhythms I grew up listening to as a child. "She copies a lot of little things from your mother," Grandma says, amused. "She always denies it though. Between you and me, I think she honestly doesn't realize she's doing it."

"Mmm," I say. Unlike my mother, I am uncomfortable discussing Aunt Miho. It's bad enough that I, a mere grandchild, have usurped her rightful place as Grandma's only remaining daughter. "This heat!" I exclaim, adjusting our shared parasol so that it shades her more fully. This solicitousness is a habit I've developed since Mother's death, partly to carry on my mother's role but also, especially in those early days, to provide an outlet for all the tenderness I never gave my mother. It seems to impress the elderly neighbors. "What a comfort your granddaughter must be, in your old age!" they say wistfully. And Grandma replies, "She's just like her mother. Sometimes I actually forget who I'm talking to."

"A! A!" Grandma now exclaims. We have just crossed Shimbonmachi Boulevard and are entering the crowded open-air market. "Good thing I remembered! Remind me, after the fish store, to buy shiso leaves for your dinner. To go with the sashimi."

Whenever I accompany Grandma to the open-air market, the fish vendor—a shrewd older woman—sidles up to us with her most expensive items. "Madam!" she greets Grandma today. "After she's back in America you'll be kicking yourself, with all due respect, for not letting her taste this highest-quality roe! At its absolute prime, madam, this time of year!"

She waits, with a complacent smile, as Grandma wavers. "Over in America," she informs my grandmother, as she wraps up our sashimi plus two other unbudgeted purchases, "those people eat their fish cooked in *butter*." She turns to me with an apologetic smile. "You sure have your granny's laugh, though," she says, exempting me from her earlier slur against Westerners. "Startles me every time, miss, coming from that American face."

It's true I bear little resemblance to anyone on my Japanese side. Sometimes I imagine Yasunari rising from the dead, and his shock and bewilderment upon seeing his own wife walking alongside a Caucasian, channeling to her all the love that was originally meant for him. But Grandma is adamant about our physical similarity. The way my thumb joins my hand, for instance, is the same as Yasunari's, and I have the same general "presence" he and my mother did. And she recently confessed that in the early days, whenever I said *"moshi moshi"* over the telephone, she would have a crazy lurch of hope that Mother's death had all been a big mistake. My voice, she insisted, was identical to my mother's.

We turn homeward onto Temple Alley, walking abreast. Three years ago this alley was gravel; now it is paved. Our summer sandals make flat, slapping sounds against the blacktop, and I miss the gentle *k'sha k'sha* that had reminded me of walking on new-fallen snow.

The houses have changed too, since my last visit: many have been rebuilt Western style, with white siding and brass doorknobs. Shiny red motor scooters are parked outside. In the middle of one door hangs a huge wooden cutout of a puppy, holding in its smiling mouth a nameplate spelling out THE MATSUDA'S in Roman letters. A bicycle bell tings behind us: we stand off to one side as a housewife rides past, straight-backed, her wire basket filled with newspaper-wrapped groceries for dinner.

"Where was that little alley that never changed?" I ask Grandma as we resume walking abreast. She gives a short, puzzled laugh as I describe the alley to her.

"I have no idea what you're talking about," she says. "Ginkgo tree? *Cicadas?* What kind of clue is that to go on?"

"There was an old-fashioned adobe wall," I say.

Grandma shakes her head, baffled. "They've torn a lot of those down." She stops short. "Meri-chan," she says, "did we remember to lock the back door when we left?"

Perhaps in the future when Grandma is gone, I will walk with my small daughter—who may have even less Japanese blood than I do—through these same neighborhood alleys. And a certain quality of reproach in the late-afternoon sunlight will remind me with a pang, as it does now, of my mother's confident voice saying, "I'm irreplaceable."

"Once, when I was a girl," I will tell my daughter, gripping her hand tightly, "I walked these alleys just like you, with my own mother." Saying these inadequate words, I will sense keenly how much falls away with time; how lives intersect but only briefly.

"Thank goodness I remembered the shiso leaves," Grandma says now. She peers over into my shopping basket. "You're always so particular about wrapping them around your *hira-masa* sushi."

"That's not me, Grandma," I say. "That was Mother."

"Oh. Well. . . ." She is silent for a moment. "That would make sense," she says. "Poor thing. It was never available during the postwar years, and she craved it for years after she moved away to . . ."

"Grandma," I interrupt gently. "It's too late for that now. It doesn't matter."

Grandma quickens her pace, as she sometimes does when she is annoyed. "One doesn't always get the luxury of timing," she says.

Circling the Hondo

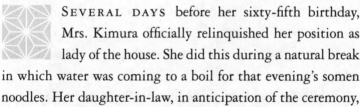SEVERAL DAYS before her sixty-fifth birthday, Mrs. Kimura officially relinquished her position as lady of the house. She did this during a natural break in which water was coming to a boil for that evening's somen noodles. Her daughter-in-law, in anticipation of the ceremony, had already taken off her apron. The entire process—the mutual bows, the long-rehearsed gracious phrases—lasted but five minutes, with only a slight sourness on Mrs. Kimura's part.

Mrs. Kimura was past her prime. There was word on the alley that (to use a local expression) a stitch or two was coming loose. Even before her change in roles, Mrs. Kimura's eyes had taken on a vague, inward cast; when she was greeted by neighbors at the open-air market, it took her just a shade too long to respond. Mrs. Kimura would pay for an expensive *aji* fillet, the fish vendor reported, only to walk off without it. Her five-year-old grandson Terao, who had grown two whole centimeters that summer, boasted that Grandma sometimes mistook him for his father. Maa maa, the neighbors could only imagine what went on in that household.

It had not been this hot and muggy in years. "Must be the global warming effect," was the Kanayagi district's greeting of choice that summer. Cicadas shrilled up in the ginkgo trees, whose leaves, sticky with dust, cast slow-stirring shadows on the pavement. Moss pushed up through cracks in the asphalt, where housewives tossed out buckets of water to cool the alley when the sun went down.

"It's all this humidity, that's what it is," Mrs. Kimura told her son, Jiro, at dinner. "It plays on everybody's mind! Ne, who can remember anything in all this heat!"

"Soh soh," he agreed from behind the evening paper. He turned a page. His wife, Harumi, shot her an inscrutable glance but said nothing.

"It gives me strange dreams at night, even," Mrs. Kimura said.

While she was lady of the house, Mrs. Kimura had rarely dreamed. Now she awoke each morning engulfed in some residual mood, which spread over the day like an expanse of calm and deepening water. Sometimes no details remained, but other times she could vaguely link her emotion to some throwaway instant from her past: the play of late-afternoon sunlight in the maple trees of a school yard, or a certain way her late husband's shadow would fall upon the wall, almost twenty years ago, when he went over finances in the evening.

looked up with sharp interest. "That's Shizu-kun's big brother!" he interrupted.

Mrs. Kimura, ignoring him, continued. "Urashimataro walked down the alley," she said, "but his old house was gone." Little Terao was listening rapt, his mouth falling open a little. "His old neighbors were gone. All of them . . . strangers." She looked over her bifocals into Terao's eyes. Their whites were clear and unveined. Limpid irises, like shallow water—she could see almost to the bottom. Terao must be imagining Urashimataro's predicament now, the way she did as a child, with the delicious thrill of momentarily leaving the safety of his own world. She marveled at his innocence, at his little mind's unawareness of all that lay around and above and beneath him. His older brother's mind, by contrast, was branching out rapidly. But he too had far to go; the expanses of time, of space, of human understanding, had yet to unfold. Mrs. Kimura felt all this vaguely, in the space of a heartbeat.

"He opened the magic box," she concluded, "and smoke poured out, and suddenly he had turned into an old man with long white beard."

The sky's familiar blue was gone now, replaced by an ominous wall of tangerine-pink. In contrast to this incandescence, the veranda below seemed suddenly darker, the boys shadowed featureless in the twilight. Little Terao was scratching at something on his arm. One flex of her mind . . . and there he would become her own son as a little boy, sitting before her on the veranda as he had done so many summers ago. It was Jiro she saw now, from a vantage point she had never known as a young mother. With a surge of emotion, she reached out and touched Terao's damp shoulder.

Outside her second-story window this morning, a crow wheeled over the pine branches, landed, then flapped away, leaving a branch swaying. The sun was out in full force already, white and shadowless. Mrs. Kimura lay perfectly still on her futon while last night's dream dissipated. There was no rush to rise. Meals were no longer her responsibility, and Harumi preferred her upstairs, out of the way, until breakfast was called.

All her life, Mrs. Kimura had been in awe of the passage of time and its powers of annihilation. Looking back across an ever-widening gulf, she had watched her earlier selves grow as implausible as incarnations in previous lives. (Had she really possessed the new body of an infant? Been madly in love?) But lately, she sensed that the past had never really receded but merely accumulated right beneath her waking mind. And now, with this onset of dreams, some barrier was giving way. For the dead were swimming back to life, the long-forgotten becoming the very now.

Downstairs, Harumi began chopping something with a jaunty rhythm (self-satisfied! Mrs. Kimura thought). Little Terao raised his voice in query. Somewhere out in the alley a bicycle bell tinged once, tinged again. Mrs. Kimura was conscious of this day already humming with a tireless grinding force, of which she was no longer a part.

"Mother-san? Mother-san?" said Harumi. "I was wondering if I could do this test on you from my book?" Harumi, in her new role as lady of the house, had bought an enormous hardcover book called *Caring for Your Aging Parents.* It was filled with lists of symptoms as well as photographs of boils, curved spines, and clouded irises. "Stand on one foot for me, please," Harumi said, "and I'll time how long you can hold it."

"What for! My balance is fine!" Mrs. Kimura said.

"Mother, please," Jiro said wearily from behind his morning paper. It was Sunday, his only day off. "Just go along with it. Please." So Mrs. Kimura submitted to the indignity while her grandsons, Saburo and Terao, ages eight and five, giggled and leaned eagerly over the low breakfast table.

Harumi was perpetually alert for suspicious developments: sniffing the air for burning smells, halting in midsentence at the hint of a cough or sneeze. More than once Mrs. Kimura had been reminded of those stonecutters she had watched as a child, patiently tap-tap-tapping until the inevitable crack appeared. "You seem a little unfocused this morning, Mother-san," her daughter-in-law said now, smiling. "Were you lost in your thoughts?" Her silver filling caught the sun and glinted brightly.

"My only thought," Mrs. Kimura said, "is a wish for peace and quiet." The boys glanced up with keen animal instinct, but the grown-ups' faces were as bland as ever.

Jiro folded his paper and stood up, knees cracking. "I'm going out for golf now," he announced.

"Golf, again?" said his wife. "In this heat?"

"Soh." Jiro cracked a grin for the first time that day. "All right then, ladies. Remember to keep your blood pressures down."

Mrs. Kimura's feelings for Jiro were complex. There was an old saying: "In youth, obey your father; in marriage, obey your husband; in old age, obey your son." It was one thing to defer to a father or husband, who from the outset commanded

respect. But the shift in power between mother and son cost them both something. Harumi's presence, most certa had not helped.

It was hard to reconcile this laconic businessman wi memory of the warm sleeping infant strapped to her b the little boy standing in the doorway, his face tear above a broken butterfly net. Or the young man, st pride, placing his very first paycheck before the fam One could not help but feel (with unease—for h Harumi's book interpret this?) that age revealed real fragmented thing.

That evening, Mrs. Kimura entertained the boys tale while their parents attended a midsummer F They sat out on the garden veranda—the boy dinner stupor, their soap-scented skin already n spiration. "So young Urashimataro descended t the sea," she said, "on the tortoise's back. Th him changed from clear to light green, then d then a deep midnight blue." She batted away her paper fan. The sun had just set, and str orange stretched across the sky as if draw brush, revealing behind its gaps the milky they reached the underwater kingdom."

Mrs. Kimura told them how, after Emperor of the Sea, Urashimataro came l find with horror that a hundred years ha bicycle passed by in the alley, flashin among the slats of the bamboo fence.

"Jiro-kun," she said.

In the dusk, Saburo snickered.

By now the color had leached from the sky. The white light of morning, the wheeling crow, was a distant memory. Even the quality of air had changed along with the fading light; she recognized in this evening the quicksilver quality, the shifting groundlessness, of her dreams. And it seemed to her that here was life's essence, revealed as it never could be in the level light of day.

"Ne, is it a true story?" asked Terao.

Saburo snorted. "Of course not!" he said.

One afternoon in late summer, the mailman delivered a parcel of high-grade *gyokuro* tea, compliments of one of Jiro's business contacts. To Mrs. Kimura, an avid tea lover, it was clear that the subtle bitterness of such a tea would be wasted on ordinary bean dumplings; it required a dessert with correspondingly subtle sweetness, like plum *yokan*.

"The open-air market?" Harumi said. "Must you go right *now,* in the middle of this heat? At your *age,* Mother-san?"

"I'm not helpless yet," Mrs. Kimura said, shaking out her parasol.

"You wait till evening," said the new lady of the house.

Anger tightened around Mrs. Kimura's chest like a vise. It was hard to breathe. "Allow me the freedom," she said coldly, "to come and go in my own house."

Harumi sighed, with that puckering of brow used by long-suffering women in samurai dramas.

Seething, Mrs. Kimura stalked down Ushigome Alley and

onto Kinjin Alley, past houses with their sliding doors half-open in hopes of a breeze. The children had gone back to school. All was silent save for the one-note shimmering of cicadas which, in its constancy, was a silence in itself. She passed an open window, where someone was washing dishes and humming behind a flowered curtain. She felt light-headed. It was hard to breathe. That Harumi! Suddenly the alley seemed to undulate in air as dense and distorting as old glass.

Slightly dizzy, Mrs. Kimura halted. Ara, where was she? Before her was an unfamiliar temple entrance flanked by two stone lions. She stumbled inside and sank down onto a nearby bench in the shade of a ginkgo tree. Black spots bloomed and shrank before her eyes. She lowered her head between her knees.

As she stayed bent over in this position, the roaring in her ears subsided and she became conscious of a distant clamor: the honk of a car, bicycle bells, the bellowing of vendors. The open-air market must be nearby. From somewhere a school bell tolled—*kinn konn kann konn*—and children's voices rose to a crescendo, then faded into stillness.

When Mrs. Kimura finally sat up, an aged man was sitting beside her in the shade. A leaf drifted down between them. "Another hot day," he said, placidly fanning himself with a pocket-size folding fan as if behavior like hers happened every day. He gestured to a water-filled paper cup on the seat between them. "From the administrative office."

Mrs. Kimura bowed her thanks, then sipped with unsteady hands. "Yes, it's gotten hot," she replied. A strand of hair had fallen loose from her bun, and she tucked it behind her ear. "It must be the global warming effect."

"Is that so," said the aged man. His voice was clear and res-onant, the voice of a younger man or even—she had the fleet-ing impression—of a spirit speaking through a medium. "Maybe," he continued, "the globe never really changes. Maybe it's just the people."

"Or their circumstances," said Mrs. Kimura. She smiled over her paper cup, pleased with that one.

"Aaa soh, madam, circumstances."

What a restful conversation. It was such a relief, compared to what she went through at home: scrambling after little facts and details, all of which came naturally to the young and gave them the upper hand in everything from avoiding oncoming bicycles to making fast replies.

They sat in silence.

"Do you live nearby?" she asked, hiding her feet, with their plastic household sandals, under the bench.

"No, no. Wakayama Prefecture. I came today by train."

Ah! She must have wandered, then, into Ko-ken-ji, a well-known local temple dedicated to the Easement of Pain. It served the blue-collar neighborhood of shopkeepers and weav-ers who made their living in the open-air market. This temple was said to attract visitors from as far away as Nagasaki—can-cer victims, arthritics, the brokenhearted—who found it out, somehow, through some underground source. Through the years, Mrs. Kimura had spotted them disembarking from buses, directions in hand: pausing dazed as straight-backed housewives whizzed past on old bicycles; as vendors bellowed for attention up and down Kanayagi Boulevard—"Fresh fish, horaa! Wel-cooome, madam! *Fresh-fresh-fish!*" She had seen them wander tentatively past shop after rickety shop, searching: past wooden barrels of yellow pickled radishes, ivory prayer beads with purple tassels, fragrant baked eels glistening with dark sauce.

What if someone today had noticed her heading toward the Temple of Pain? People would be interested. They would talk among themselves. She is no longer lady of the house, they would say.

Out in the street a motor scooter sputtered past, its noise gradually fading into the distant buzz of the open-air market. She should be getting along. Which way was it to the open-air market? Never before had Mrs. Kimura lost her way like this. She felt an onset of dread which, lately, was becoming familiar. She glanced over at the old man who clearly could not help her, being from Wakayama Prefecture. He was settled on the bench, still fanning himself. This is where I belong, his posture seemed to say. Without his marvelous voice the aged body looked smaller, dried up and scrawny like a grasshopper—yet with something of that concealed energy of grasshoppers, that ability to startle you with a leap bigger than their bodies were entitled to.

Now, with a slow movement, he lifted his arm and pointed at a shabby wooden temple about a hundred meters away. "I was circling the *hondo*," he told her. Lined up along the temple's veranda was evidence of a large attendance: glass jars, dozens and dozens of them, scrubbed clean of labels and crammed with homegrown carnations, sweet peas, dahlias. They seemed to belong to an intimate household whose owners could return at any time.

"At the administrative office," he said, "I bought one hundred sticks blessed by a priest. Then I circled the *hondo* one hundred times, reciting the Lotus Sutra to myself. After each round, I dropped one stick in the box."

Poor man. Mrs. Kimura, distracted from her own worries, nodded with sympathy. This ritual sounded strangely familiar. There had been something in her own past—what it was, she could not recall.

"I went round and round. And the process began to remind me of all the years of my life. How they've come and gone. You go around enough times, and it all gets blurred together. Isn't that the way, madam? Things lose their shape."

Mrs. Kimura sat up straighter but said nothing.

"But what's the point now of clutching at all the dates and names and places? I thought, Let them go! Let them go! They've served their purpose. —Madam, while I was circling the *hondo* I paused to hear the cicadas. I stood and listened, and I felt an old man inside me, and a middle-aged man too, and a young man, and a boy."

Overhead in the branches, one of the cicadas stopped shrilling, then started up again. Mrs. Kimura thought back to the evening several weeks ago, when she had sat on the veranda with her grandsons and sensed the difference in their minds' respective capacities. Now, she felt her role reversed; this old man had captured something that still eluded her, although it was encroaching closer and closer from the edges of her mind.

"Imagine how cicadas would sound to Buddha," he said, "after all his incarnations."

Was he, then, a religious follower? "I don't believe in re-incarnation," Mrs. Kimura said.

"Saa, I'm not sure myself," he said, "what happens after death. But I see its pattern in this life. The ancient sages said we all have in us some larger consciousness that keeps growing, widening, with time. And they said: That is all that matters. Our bodies must evolve, and our minds must evolve, in order to accommodate it."

It was not until the old man had left for his train that Mrs. Kimura remembered why the *hondo* ritual had sounded familiar. The memory came back to her untried, utterly unfamiliar, as if it belonged in someone else's mind and was slipping into hers by mistake. It was strange, how certain pockets of memory disappeared early in life. A few of them were coming back through her dreams. Others remained missing; for instance, she could not recall a single moment of that period in childhood when she had been forced to learn how to write with her right hand.

It had been a muggy summer day—she was about six— when she and her parents had visited a temple and her father had circled a *hondo*. It must have been his cancer, Mrs. Kimura thought now. But on that day she knew nothing of this, and had become impatient waiting for him. While cicadas shrilled *meeeeee* up in the pine trees, her mother amused her with a Water Buddha in a corner of the yard. "Ahhh, he's saying thank you, it feels very good," her mother had said as she poured water from a bamboo dipper over the Buddha's head, "the poor thing's so hot and tired out in the sun." Mrs. Kimura had watched the gentle stone face smiling through a film of cool water that flowed down the Buddha's body into the tangled green weeds at its feet. Her mother poured over and over, and her father continued his interminable rounds.

They might have come to this very temple. It was not so implausible; her childhood town of Fukuma was no more than an hour away.

Mrs. Kimura pictured her father sitting on a bench, slumped and silent, and her mother bending over him saying, "Oto-san, here's some tea . . . let's rest here a little before we go home . . ." A few elderly people had sat nearby, discussing ailments and families and times long gone, slowly fanning themselves as if they had all the time in the world. One solitary old woman sipped her tea, holding the cup with both hands and smiling up eagerly at anyone passing by.

They were all gone now, and Mrs. Kimura had taken their place. That afternoon could have happened just yesterday, a heartbeat ago. Was it an illusion, or was today's weather, even the time of day, exactly the same, right down to the ominous black shafts of shadow the *hondo*'s pillars threw across the sand?—as if nothing had really happened in the meantime, as if she had blinked once, like Urashimataro, and found decades gone.

For a fleeting instant her mind was vast enough, strong enough, to inhabit both afternoons at once. Maybe those ancient sages had experienced something similar, hovering between one consciousness and another. And Buddha himself, after all those lives—a tree, a worm, a bird, a dog—was now all dimensions in one, *was all*—and something of this was coming to her in these newfound dreams, and in the twilight evenings when she reclaimed young Jiro from the past. She knew her mind to be strengthening, widening, in a way neither little Terao nor Saburo nor Harumi nor Jiro could hope to understand.

She rose from her seat and walked over to the Water Buddha, which was still standing—as she had known it would be—in the far-left corner of the yard. It looked unexpectedly dilapidated, a little worn statue with features blurred by the years. She gazed at the smooth face, almost alive in the flickering shade of the sycamore tree. It was a face spent of passion after so many incarnations, suspended in some vast, unfocused awareness that radiated from its simple features. Mrs. Kimura, squatting before it as if it were a small child, recognized in its smile her own sorrow of things passing.

"There, there," she said to the Water Buddha, lifting the dipper and scooping up water from the blue plastic bucket beside it. The water slid down the warm stone, raising a sharp whiff of moss as it sank into the ground.

Mirror Studies

THE KASHIGAWA district, two hours away from the Endos' home in Tokyo, was an isolated farming community with two claims to distinction: indigenous harrier monkeys up in the hills, and a new restaurant—Fireside Rations—which served "rice" made from locally grown yams. This restaurant had been featured in an *Asahi Shimbun* article about the trendy resurgence of wartime food, also known as nostalgia cuisine, and it had received special mention on NHK's thirty-minute *Rural Getaways* show. City dwellers, jaded by French and Madeiran cuisine, were flocking out on weekends to try it. It seemed a fitting place for Dr. Kenji Endo; his wife, Sumiko; and Dr. Ogawa to toast the start of a new primate field study.

This field study would be Kenji's last. Sumiko had insisted on it, quoting the doctor about the seriousness of his arrhythmia. "There's enough work for you at the university," she said, "where you'll have access to phones and doctors." Kenji had conceded with ill humor. Even now, at odd moments, that decision pressed hard on his chest, where he felt his heart galumphing under the skin. He was lucky, he supposed, to have this last project, a mere thirty-minute drive from this small town of Kashigawa. It would require almost no physical exertion; he had deliberately confined his mirror experiments to the provisioning area where monkeys came to feed.

Tonight, dressing for dinner at the Red Monkey Inn, Kenji stood behind his wife, who was fluffing her hair before the vanity mirror, and faced his own reflection. It pleased him that at fifty-eight he still looked good, belying the heart condition that, despite medication or perhaps because of it, had drained him over the past three months ("What happened to those pompous monologues of yours?" a close friend had joked recently). He was permanently tanned from years of working in the wilds of Borneo and Madagascar, and beneath his pressed spring suit he retained the lithe frame and hard calves of a trekker. Unlike Dr. Ogawa, whom they were meeting tonight, Kenji still had a full head of salt-and-pepper hair that he parted in a dashing side sweep each morning. His only visible symptom of age was a tendency to walk or stand with knees slightly bent: the first sign of a curved back, according to his secretary at the university. He always caught himself, therefore, and corrected it immediately.

"I'd forgotten," his wife remarked, "how common yams are in Kashigawa. I'm surprised we didn't get one in our welcome basket." She smiled enigmatically at her reflection, turning her profile this way and that. Sumiko had grown up on the west side of this district, in a small hamlet long since swallowed up by postwar suburbs. Secure in her own sophistication, she often amused their city friends with anecdotes from her rural childhood.

"The monkeys today sure liked them, ne?" Kenji said. Ordinarily, he discussed primates for hours on end—anytime, with anyone—but lately this tendency had abated. He found himself economizing in other ways as well: if he needed a book from another room, he put off rising from his chair until it was time to use the bathroom; he sat silent in the chair while working through a complex thought process, rather than pacing the room and talking aloud as he was accustomed. He sensed how this slower pace hampered his creativity, his greatest asset, and this realization also lay heavy on his chest. For so long now, his mental agility—augmented by his affiliation with the nation's most elite university, and a long and respected publishing career—had cleared his every path like a red carpet. As a young man, naturally, he had battled hard for advancement. But that was decades ago; until the advent of his arrhythmia, he could barely remember how it felt to be thwarted.

On this particular evening, however, Kenji was in fine form. He was eager to talk. His thoughts sprang up, keen and full-bodied, like stringed notes plucked by a koto master. He had felt this way for two whole days now, and he harbored a secret hope that his heart problems were receding as mysteriously as they had once appeared. Luckier things had happened in his lifetime. "Did you notice," he said, "how they peeled the yams with their incisors, then washed them in the stream?"

"Aaa, aaa," Sumiko agreed, "you showed me." She powdered her nose, leaning in close to the mirror. "Like miniature housewives," she said, "with those little black dexterous hands."

There was an emotional hardiness about Sumiko that Kenji assumed came from her country stock or—more likely—from being married to him. He had always appreciated this quality in her, like a rope on which he, the mountain climber, could entrust his full weight. "I'm a research widow," she had mourned jokingly in their early years, as Kenji departed for one exotic locale after another. "Wave bye-bye to Papa-san," she told their toddler, Toji, carrying him in one arm and demonstrating with the other. After Toji entered high school, she immediately joined several women's committees; the experience had added a gloss of poise to her unruffled core. "A charming woman!" people often said of Kenji's wife.

"Their food washing is learned behavior," Kenji told her. "It's one of the brightest discoveries credited to Japanese researchers."

"Aaa," Sumiko murmured, blotting her lipstick with a tissue.

"Because it's proto-tool use, you see, which is a key component of human culture."

This afternoon's tour of the site had been brief, just to confirm all was in order. Dr. Ogawa and his assistant, who were actually here on a project of their own, had been kind enough to set up Kenji's freestanding mirror for him, the two men lugging it up the dirt trail and propping it securely in the middle of the clearing. The monkeys would have unlimited access to this mirror before official tests were performed; this would allow plenty of time for them to establish familiarity with it.

"In the first mirror study eleven years ago," Kenji explained to Dr. Ogawa later that evening at the restaurant, "a few orangutans actually showed signs of self-recognition. The same with chimpanzees. An exciting discovery! But then that study of Japanese snow monkeys, headed by my friend Itakura—do you know Itakura?"

Dr. Ogawa, who dealt with physiology rather than cognitive behavior, did not. But he had run across articles.

"Well, anyhow, that study was a disappointment. The monkeys interpreted the reflections to be either other members of the same species or else meaningless images. So the obvious question is—"

"Is there a rift between monkey and ape," Sumiko provided, rummaging in her handbag and pulling out a handkerchief.

"—soh soh, exactly. Whether it indicates a major evolutionary discontinuity."

"Fascinating," breathed Dr. Ogawa's assistant.

"I think it's pretty early for a conclusion like *that,*" said Dr. Ogawa.

Kenji halted him with a raised forefinger, nodding. Absolutely, he said. There were so many unexplored variables. Some apes, such as gorillas, showed no self-recognition whatsoever. He personally suspected some correlation between a species's level of aggression and its concept of self. "Wouldn't aggression be the natural result," he said, "of a capacity for self-awareness being developed and adapted for survival?" These Kashigawa monkeys represented a strain of macaque which was, with the exception of baboons, one of the most ferocious in the entire primate family. He hoped this characteristic would make for some interesting findings.

"On what grounds?" Dr. Ogawa asked.

"It's still a hunch at this stage," Kenji said. A good many such hunches had paid off during his career. Much of this, he knew, was sheer luck, but surely some of the credit went to a scientist's gift for inventiveness, for subconscious mental connections. He loved telling the story of Einstein, whose theory of relativity had begun with a childish fantasy of riding on a beam of light. "I have some latitude to explore as I go," he now said.

"Aggression studies must be 'in' again," Dr. Ogawa said grimly. "Psychologists, sociologists, they're all whipped up about it."

Kenji laughed. He felt invincible tonight, closer to his old self than he had been in a while; he was conscious that every good hour, indeed every good minute, was ensuring his odds of recovery. "Our nation has a hunger to understand," he explained, forearms leaning heavily on the dinner table as if it were a podium, "given our experience with the most destructive war in modern history, what seed within humans made it possible. We can look back now from the safe distance of time. Even this wartime cuisine—I think it's all part of the process."

Dr. Ogawa, a middle-aged medical man with little regard for trends of the masses and even less for culinary fads, drank his Asahi beer and looked skeptical. He was here on a project of his own: collecting DNA samples for a study of pathogens and sialic acids, a process that led him and his assistant far out into the hills with their stun guns. Dr. Ogawa vaguely reminded Kenji of alpha male apes he had studied in the past.

Not in any aggressive sense, but rather in the quiet force of his linear focus, that unrelenting, almost brute push of each thought to the very end. Kenji looked forward to some interesting debates. He knew from a colleague that Dr. Ogawa was fairly well known within physiology circles.

"Sohh sohh, wartime cuisine," sighed Dr. Ogawa's assistant, a weary-eyed graduate student whom Dr. Ogawa perversely addressed by the babyish nickname of Kana-chan. "We're simply inundated with it," he said, with a prim moue of distaste comically identical to Dr. Ogawa's.

Kenji laughed out loud at this, slapped his thigh. His exuberance had been rising all evening. His heartbeat was returning to normal—yes! he could sense it, with that intuition for success that had seldom failed him in the past. "You're absolutely right!" he said generously. Speaking of war cuisine, he told the table, two *okonomiyaki* places had sprung up in his own neighborhood. Kenji, having grown up in the city during the war and the occupation that followed, remembered those crispy pancakes: meager substitutes for rationed rice, their flour content barely enough to bind together leftover scraps of cabbage or turnip stems. Nowadays, of course, such ingredients were upgraded for modern consumption.

"Rock shrimp! Calamari! *Filet mignon!*" Kenji crowed. "They've missed the entire point!"

His audience laughed appreciatively, the assistant most heartily of all.

"Way before your time, Kana-chan," Dr. Ogawa teased, patting the young man's shoulder. Kana-chan flushed and stopped laughing.

Their waiter approached. In the muted candlelight (Kenji

took out his reading glasses), they peered down at the identical bowls set before them. Yam rice, the waiter said, was unique to this region. First, yams were mashed. Binding glutens were added, and the mixture was strained through a large-holed colander into boiling water. The resulting noodlelike strands, once cooked, were chopped into rice-size bits. These were bleached, then finally roasted.

"All that work," murmured Sumiko, "just so they could pretend they were eating rice." The rice had a chewy, nutty texture not unlike that of brown rice, although its flavor was largely masked by salt and azuki beans.

From nowhere, a familiar tiredness hit Kenji. The shock and disappointment of it paralyzed him; he had put so much faith in this comeback. He sat still, feeling himself descending in slow motion beneath the bright surface of the dinner conversation, as if to the bottom of a sea.

With this underwater sensation, which so often accompanied his fluctuations in blood flow, he gazed dully at his wife sitting before him. She was eating slowly, pensively, deep in a world of her own. He recalled her saying once at a dinner party that her own mother, who had died when Sumiko was in middle school, used to reminisce about eating yam rice while she was pregnant with Sumiko. He wondered if his wife was remembering this now. It was strange how these small shifts in blood flow could open him up to the sadness of things, like a receding tide exposing sea creatures crumpled on the sand. His wife's way of eating this dish struck him as profound, an acknowledgment of all the loss and longing that had created it.

"Think of all the labor they could have saved," Kana-chan was saying, "if they'd just baked their yams instead."

Tiredness poured in from all sides now, like sand into a hole, infusing Kenji with an unaccustomed sense of disadvantage. The new generation, he thought. Never gone hungry, never had a familiar world jerked out from under their feet. Before this young mind, as hard and green as an unripe peach, Kenji felt unaccountably uneasy.

"Irregular heartbeats have various causes," Kenji's doctor had told him at the beginning. "For example, minuscule heart attacks can build up scar tissue over time, which interferes with electrical impulses."

"But I have excellent arteries. My blood pressure, my cholesterol, everything's in a good range!"

"Well, then," the doctor said—briskly, as if nipping a pointless argument in the bud—"yours must be hereditary. These flaws do crop up in later years, and we can't always explain them."

It was unnerving to think how confidently he had stridden through life, utterly ignorant of what defects lurked in his genes. Today, months later, Kenji mulled it over again, sitting at the edge of the dirt clearing and observing the macaques. Five or six of them, sated from a lunch of yams, loitered thirty meters away, grooming each other or strolling about on all fours. Directly overhead the sumac leaves rustled, intermittently letting in a blinding flash of sun. Kenji closed his eyes— it was just for a moment, the monkeys were nowhere near the mirror—and orange flooded his eyelids, the warmth pressing down on his face and body like a blanket. He felt great solace in the midst of this loudness that was nature: the back-and-forth of birds, the drilling of a woodpecker, the alternate drone and *chi-chi-chi* of insects, the grunt of a monkey.

How he would miss fieldwork: this riotous energy all about him, each cell living with all its might, yet synchronized in cycles of deceptive efficiency.

Kenji's fascination with nature had started when he was six, when his family had evacuated to the countryside to stay with relatives after the Namiki bombing. He still looked back on those months as the finest in his childhood. One day his granny had taken him to a dense pine thicket to pick shiitake mushrooms with other villagers, wicker baskets slung over their backs. They had all roared with good-natured laughter whenever someone forgot and leaned over too far, causing the contents of his basket to come tumbling out. . . .

"Everything in nature is put here on purpose," his granny had told him, pushing apart mushrooms as soft as flesh, "to keep something else alive. Nature knows exactly what it's doing." And the boy, young as he was, had grasped something of this omniscient bounty. He felt secure and protected on those rainy nights when they all hunched over the brazier, mouths watering over roasted mushrooms and quail eggs.

Later, as a young man, Kenji attempted to re-create the wonder of those early days by studying the natural sciences, which promised ever-widening vistas of discovery. His focus on primate sociology was a lucky accident—the influence of a particularly charismatic mentor—or so he had always believed. But in the past few months, as he looked back over his career, it had occurred to Kenji that his specialty was a logical, if somewhat extreme, extension of his nostalgia for living off the land. In primate society was the essence of oneness with nature that humans must once have had, muddied now by all the ills of modern life. At this late age, Kenji felt a rueful tenderness for his early idealism; and in this context, perhaps, he had become unduly disheartened during yesterday's talk with Dr. Ogawa.

Over the past few weeks, the two men had held some interesting discussions as they drove into town in the evenings (Kana-chan had to stay behind, sorting specimens). Both Kenji and Dr. Ogawa were interested in the concept of evolutionary divergence.

"New studies tell us," Dr. Ogawa had said, as they descended past terrace after terrace of rice paddies darkening in the twilight, "that human DNA is almost identical to that of primates. Almost *identical*. How is this possible? What accounts, then, for the vast difference between the species?"

A few months ago, Kenji would have made an irreverent quip about not being so sure there *was* a vast difference, following it up with various conjectures of his own. Since the yam rice dinner, however, his old economy had returned. This evening, weary, he merely shook his head with a *hnn* sound.

"Sialic acids," Dr. Ogawa said with quiet relish. "That's one of the clues." Characteristic of his step-by-step thought process, he started at the beginning. Sialic acids acted as a protective layer over a species's DNA structure, shielding it from invasion and alteration by outside viruses. It had been discovered, only recently, that human sialic acids had a makeup distinctly different from that of primates'.

"Which would suggest," Dr. Ogawa said, "that each species was influenced, over time, by different viruses."

Dr. Ogawa's theory was this: long ago, in humans, some

virus had tampered with the delicate balance of electrical impulses that prevents every mammalian brain from exceeding its predetermined size limit. "So now humans are born with open sutures in the skull," Dr. Ogawa said, "to accomodate further brain growth. Whereas every other mammal continues to be born with a fully knit skull."

"So what you're saying," Kenji said dully, "is that our larger brains, our self-awareness, basically everything that makes us human, is in direct violation of nature's internal control system?"

"Maa maa, Endo-san, isn't that a dire interpretation! Evolution is all *about* mutation."

Kenji could sense his own brain firing, working, but in that slow underwater way, the clean lines of scientific thought tangling in the kelp of his personal sorrows. "A mutation like this would have enormous repercussions," he said finally. "It casts a whole new light on humans running amok over the biosphere. The human brain as the supreme anomaly, a divine defect. . . ." A sense of futility had washed over him, and in spite of himself he sought Dr. Ogawa's eyes for reassurance.

Dr. Ogawa's eyes, squinting suspiciously behind their lenses, seemed small and far away, as if seen from the other end of a telescope. "Defect? What, like de-evolution? What kind of unscientific talk is that?"

"Viruses, too, thrive by ravaging their own environment," Kenji said. In the deepening dusk, the dirt road glowed whitely before them.

"Interesting. I suppose one *could* find similarities." Dr. Ogawa turned his headlights on. "But why make moral judgments about life-forms?"

A woodpecker, drilling directly above his head, brought Kenji back to the present. He opened his eyes. His recent problems suddenly seemed alien compared to the sunny scene before him, tasseled grasses waving and everything in perfect harmony down to the *pyoo pyoo* of a whitetail: one giant attuned orchestra. He had a fleeting impression that his arrhythmia was the consequence of straying so far, over the decades, from the simple faith he had once known as a boy. How much this career of his had cost him: the joys of a simple home life, the bonds he might have forged with a son, now grown and distant in Wakayama.

One of the monkeys, a young male, had ambled over to the mirror and now sat hunched before it with his back to Kenji, unmoving. Typical beta behavior, he thought automatically. An alpha would have charged the mirror or bared its teeth. But in another few weeks they would all be sitting sideways before the mirror, monitoring the scene by glancing back and forth between the clearing and the reflected image.

Kenji could make out the monkey's close-set eyes in the freestanding mirror, peering unblinkingly at its small reddened face. Seen from the rear he looked pitifully human, tiny shoulder blades poking up through the fur, and Kenji had the same urge he used to have when his son was small, to rest his hand on that narrow back. Primates moved him, as did children, by all they were incapable of understanding.

When Kenji came home (they had by now transferred from Red Monkey Inn to a condominium, with its veranda overlooking Kashigawa Valley), his wife was boiling something in the kitchen. Its pungent, earthy smell hit him as soon as he opened the door.

"They're wild *fuki* shoots from the hills, where your monkeys are," Sumiko told him. She looked excited and happy. "A woman at the market gave me the recipe." Her hair was wrapped up, peasant-style, in one of the dyed indigo kerchiefs native to the area. Her dark-skinned face, washed clean of cosmetics and glistening from the heat of the stove, put him in mind of the healthy country women of his childhood.

"Ara, you're cooking!" he said in mock surprise. "What's going on? Is this the latest in country chic?"

She gave an embarrassed little laugh, pulling off her new kerchief as she did so, and once again she was the university wife from Tokyo. "So how's your new medication working?" she asked, businesslike.

"So-so," Kenji said. He couldn't help an inward cringe; his condition was a fragile thing, to be cradled in the soft recesses of his mind and handled, only at the right time and with utmost delicacy, by no one but himself.

"Try not to get your hopes up," Sumiko said. "Remember what the doctor said? That a certain level of fatigue is probably unavoidable?"

"Aaa, aaa, right."

"Try to be more careful about long hours, and don't run yourself down. Remember, you have a serious condition."

"Aaa! Aaa!" He escaped to the bathroom for his predinner bath, which was ready and steaming under its heavy lid. Sumiko had purchased some old-fashioned gourd loofahs, as well as an array of local beauty products. Kenji picked up, then put down, a small jar of soy curd, labeled "The Beauty Lotion of Our Mothers." It was unseemly, an intelligent woman like Sumiko embracing this wartime trend like she was a member of the masses. It occurred to him, briefly, to wonder about her day-to-day life, so closely linked to his and yet riddled with mysterious gaps. He tried imagining it: a slower pace, a narrower scope, the kind of world he himself had always resisted.

Settled in his bath now, his mind restfully blank, Kenji gazed down at his body wavering beneath the shifting water. It always came as something of a jar, after a full day of observing primates, to view the naked human form: the vestigial shortness of the arms, the pink hairless skin, vulnerable and fetuslike.

Evolution is all about mutation.

That talk with Dr. Ogawa had, since then, vaguely reminded Kenji of another scientist, and he now remembered, with the satisfying click of a fact falling into place, who it was. Buffon—a French naturalist from the eighteenth century—had proposed that humans, biologically speaking, were born at least a year too soon. Kenji had read him many years ago, in the context of another topic which he could not recall, and at the time he had found the man's claims entertaining but not particularly relevant to his work. Buffon claimed that man was forced to complete, within society, a psychological development that all other species accomplished within the womb. As Kenji recalled, this had to do with the human head being too large to be carried full term. Man's problems, apparently, traced back to this prematurity of birth.

Buffon's idea had been bolstered by another European—Ludwig Bolk, from the 1920s—who proved that mutations inhibiting maturation did occur naturally in animals.

Kenji closed his eyes and conjured up the perfection of this afternoon: the sound of leaves and insects and birds weaving together into one drowsy murmur, the monkeys seated on the ground, gnawing on yams with their hairy legs splayed out before them. Like Eden, according to the Western conception: the paradise from which man was banished almost immediately after his creation. Kenji recalled that Christianity, unlike the Eastern religions, believed humans to be distinct from animals, born under a shadow of original sin. Well, perhaps they had tapped into something. Clues were everywhere. How odd that he had never noticed.

"Dinner's ready!" called Sumiko from the hallway.

Unfortunately, Kenji's new medication brought on proarrhythmia, an exacerbation of his preexisting condition. "Saa, who knows why?" his doctor said blandly, ignoring Kenji's glare of exasperated disgust. "Every so often, antiarrhythmic drugs have tricky side effects." An appointment was made for a pacemaker installation.

The operation was to take place in three days. This afternoon, sprawled in a chair on the condominium terrace, Kenji mulled over the mirror test that he planned to administer tomorrow. It was the first and most basic of the series: anesthetizing the monkeys, painting green dye on their heads, then seeing if the recovered monkeys touched their own heads while looking in the mirror.

It worried him that, after almost two months of loose observation, he had come up with no significant brainstorms, unusual connections, or inspirations for more tailored tests. Loose observation was usually his most fertile period, when chance details coupled with spontaneous insights guided the course of his study, refining a general hunch into a testable hypothesis. But this time, although he earnestly, even desperately, watched the monkeys grooming or fingering the mirror or leaping lightly from branch to branch, nothing clicked into place. He was like a thick-witted detective at a crime scene, unable to make sense of clues right before his eyes.

Never mind, Kenji told himself. He gave a curt sigh and glanced at his watch. It was a little after four. In a few hours, his new assistant from the university, whom he had recruited to handle the monkey anesthetization as well as any lifting or dragging, would be coming by to go over the checklist.

"I still don't see why you can't put off your experiment until we get back from Tokyo," Sumiko said. She was sitting beside him on the terrace, alternately squinting at an instruction manual and weaving something out of rattan.

With one hand, Kenji brushed away her words as if they were flies. She's like Ogawa, he thought with a flare of helpless fury. A horse with blinders.

They sat silent. The terrace overlooked the south end of Kashigawa Valley, and the cluttered towns lay faint and ephemeral in the dense daze. To Kenji's left loomed the hills of his final project, so close he could distinguish the colors of certain trees. Despite the patchwork of lime-colored rice paddies encroaching on their lower regions, the hills gave off an ancient air, as if they had never been shadowed by anything but clouds and an occasional red hawk.

After some time, Kenji glanced over at his wife. Her arm, weaving the rattan stalk in and out, moved as serenely as a swimmer's.

"What are you making?" he asked.

"A pouch," she replied, "for hard-boiled eggs."

"Aaa."

They fell silent once more. Below them in the valley a train whistle sliced the air, echoing the mournful, delayed quality of Kenji's mind.

"The first time I ever rode the slow train," Sumiko said, "my mother packed hard-boiled eggs in a straw pouch. We peeled them on the train, and ate them." She said this absently, unmindful of his response, as a mother might talk to herself in the company of a child. Kenji felt himself freeze as he instinctively did before creatures in the wild, peacefully eating and as yet unaware of a human presence.

"The window was open, the breeze was blowing in," Sumiko continued, "and you could smell the iron heated up by the sun. We were so hungry in those days. And the eggs tasted so *good,* with a sprinkle of salt. It was a wonderful day."

"Is that why you're making this bag?"

His wife looked up, suddenly self-conscious. She regarded him for a moment, with dark eyes as unfathomable as a primate's. "I thought it might be nice to take a train ride," she said. "Just for a couple of stops."

Kenji was jolted out of his own self-regard. His no-nonsense wife of thirty years, with her dinner party conversations—how long had she harbored such longings? He pictured her sitting alone by the window (did train windows even open anymore?), a woman past middle age, peeling an egg. He remembered her eating yam rice at the restaurant, and he felt a pity so deep he could not tell where it ended and his arrhythmia began.

"June is nice here in Kashigawa," he said gently. Then, after a pause, "I know what you mean. . . . When I was a boy, I once picked mushrooms in the forest." Nodding, his wife resumed her handicraft. They said no more.

This is married life, thought Kenji. Suddenly his underwater state seemed not so much a banishment but the entering of a new realm, with the slowly dawning kinship of divers who swim among the fish. In him welled up a strong allegiance with Sumiko, with his entire aging generation reaching back for their simple beginnings. What countless private Edens they had managed to extract from the war. . . .

Sumiko got up to attend to something in the kitchen. Kenji remained sitting, in the evening light which now slanted low over the hills and cast pink shadows on the valley haze. And as effortlessly as the spreading light—not with the clean scientific click of old, but with a soft suffusion—his allegiance widened out over his entire flawed race, with its fierce need to create beauty for itself.

A memory floated up in his mind. Madagascar, early in his career: towering stone crags whose jagged outcroppings snapped beneath his boots with high-pitched pings, and below them, the famous sunken forests where lemurs lived. The forests had been created, millions of years ago, by earth collapsing into itself for kilometers around, destroying all life in its wake and forever changing the land's topography. Kenji was a young man, and the forest's lush beauty had astonished him.

"Isn't life a resilient force," one senior member of their party had remarked as the scientists gazed upward in wonder, faces tinted green from the virgin foliage, "turning the worst of its disasters into something like this."